If He Only Knew

MICHELYNN CHRISTY

. . . .

BRANDI GABRIEL

Other Books Available by Michelynn Christy

A Christmas to Remember
Love Unawares

Other Books Available by Brandi Gabriel

The Orphan Bride
The Cowhand's Bride

Prologue

It happened many years ago, in 1968, to be exact. I'd just turned eighteen and Bobby and I were so in love. Or, so I'd thought.

I was the good girl. The one who always followed the rules and obeyed Momma and Daddy. My sister, on the other hand, was a different story. While she certainly wasn't the worst sinner on the block, she did manage to find her share of trouble – many times dragging me into it. But, of course, Daddy always knew I was the innocent one...

One

Preacher Benjamin Peterson briefly locked eyes with his wayward daughter Pamela and then glanced at some of the other young men and women in the congregation. "Listen closely to the following passage, brothers and sisters, and heed the warning." He glanced down at his Bible on the pulpit – likely the same pulpit his father and grandfather had preached from in decades past.

"First Corinthians chapter six, verses nine and ten read, *Know ye not that the unrighteous shall not inherit the kingdom of God? Be not deceived: neither fornicators, nor idolaters, nor adulterers, nor effeminate, nor abusers of themselves with mankind, Nor thieves, nor covetous, nor drunkards, nor revilers, nor extortioners, shall inherit the kingdom of God.* The message is clear, brothers and sisters. If we want the blessings of God, we must live a life that is pleasing to Him."

A bead of perspiration formed at his hairline, then rolled down Preacher Peterson's forehead. *Why did the air conditioner have to give out on one of the hottest days of the year?* He silently complained to God. He'd need to have one of the deacons take a look at it this week.

He finished up his sermon, which he'd purposely shortened, and gladly sat back down. A nice meal sounded great right about now. What would the girls prepare for lunch today? His girls...

Pamela had been out all hours of the night. He'd known it as soon as he heard her boyfriend's vehicle drive away. He would have gotten up to reprimand her if he hadn't been so dog tired. He'd tossed and turned all night with nary a merciful wink.

When would his daughter ever learn any sense? Didn't she realize that staying out late with young men was not a good idea? Why couldn't she just be like Donna? If only her older sister could rub off on her. He feared she'd get herself into trouble – trouble that would shame the whole family and ruin his ministerial authority. Who would respect a minister who couldn't even keep his own house in order? Nobody, that's who. If only Margaret were still here. What advice would she have offered concerning their daughters?

He'd have to have a talk with Pamela. The sooner the better for all their sakes.

....

"Pammy, wait for me!" Donna called out as her sister headed down the street on foot.

Pamela turned and sighed. "Let me guess. Daddy asked you to keep an eye on me, right?"

Donna couldn't lie so she remained silent.

"That's what I thought." Pamela shook her head. "You know I wouldn't do anything to get myself in trouble."

Donna's brow shot up. "You don't think staying out late with Danny is asking for trouble?"

"No way. Danny's a goody-two-shoes like you. He'd never do anything to get me in trouble."

"I don't know about that. Getting home after eleven? Doesn't he know your curfew is at ten?"

Pamela chewed her bottom lip and quirked a sly grin. "No, he doesn't, actually. I told him it was midnight, so he actually thinks he's bringing me home early. I told you, he's a goody-goody."

Donna gasped. "Why would you tell him that?"

"I don't want him to think I'm a baby. A ten o'clock curfew?" Pamela shook her head. "Who has a curfew of ten o'clock?"

"We do."

"Just because Daddy's the minister doesn't mean we have to miss out on all the fun."

"There's fun to be had before ten," Donna insisted.

Pamela rolled her eyes. "The stars are barely out at ten. You can't walk along the beach and look up at the stars if there are none out. If Momma were still here, I bet she'd let me stay out longer."

"You don't know that. Besides, she's not here. Daddy's all we got." The thought made Donna yearn for her mother even more. Momma's sudden death had left such a gaping hole in their family, but she was grateful to still have Daddy. She'd thought many times, that she was certain she and Pamela had the best parents in the world.

....

Donna's heart raced as Bobby Dillon's gentle fingers slid from her cheek to her neck. His lips pressed hers once again and she felt herself yielding helplessly to his desires. Bobby's hands moved down her back and he pulled her closer, his kiss deepening.

"Donna..." His voice broke with more kisses. "Let's..."

Donna knew that if she didn't put an abrupt end to Bobby's progression, they'd both do something they would later regret. She suddenly realized they were all alone and she scolded herself for being careless.

"Bobby, we shouldn't be doing this." She managed to break away but Bobby was persistent. *Temptation is an easy thing to give in to, so don't put yourself in a position where you must yield.* She remembered Momma's words.

"I can't," she heard herself say. "It wouldn't be right. What would Daddy say?"

"C'mon, Donna. Just 'cause you're the preacher man's daughter, doesn't mean you can't have a little fun once in a while. It ain't like your folks never had any fun when they were our age." His eyes beckoned her. "Besides, you know I aim to marry you someday."

"You do?" Hadn't she envisioned that very thing dozens of times over the past year? This was the first time Bobby had brought the subject of marriage up, although they'd been dating for nearly a year. Was he finally contemplating the idea? The day she and Bobby married would be a joyful one indeed. But when would *someday* be?

"There's no other girl for me but you, Donna. You know it." The sweet words rolled off his tongue and he gently grazed her shoulder with his lips. "We'll be careful, I promise." He whispered.

Donna scooted a couple of inches away from him on the love seat. "Bobby, you know I'm not *that kind* of girl."

"I know that. You're special. Why do you think I want you all for myself?" He brought her fingertips to his lips.

Donna shook her head. "No."

"Oh, Donna. You're killing me, babe."

"What if your folks come home?"

"They're at my little brother's ball game. It'll be at least a couple of hours before they return." He stroked her hair. "Besides, we'll be in my room. I have a lock on my door."

Is he really asking this of me? Finally, Donna stood up. She *really* needed to leave before Bobby's persuasion skills could win out. "I can't, Bobby."

"Why do you keep rejecting me, Donna?"

Is that what he thinks? "I'm not rejecting you, Bobby. I want to wait until it's proper."

"Proper? I'm not sure I catch your drift, Donna."

"I just want to wait, okay? Please take me home now."

"But, Donna–" He shrugged half-heartedly then sighed. "Okay."

Bobby was quiet the entire ride home. She'd offended him. "Bobby–"

"Please, Donna, I don't want to talk about it."

"If we're going to do that, we need to be married first."

Bobby rolled his eyes. "That's your father talking."

"I want to please God. Don't you, Bobby?"

"Yeah, sure." He shrugged.

"Do you really *want* to marry me, Bobby?" Could he read the doubt she felt in her heart?

"You know I do, Donna! Why would you even say that?"

"Well..." Her voice trailed off. How could she ask him why he hadn't proposed to her yet – or even mentioned marriage before today, for that matter? It wasn't her place to do the asking. They were eighteen already – plenty old enough. Momma was just seventeen when she married Daddy.

"If it's the ring you're concerned about, I've been saving up money." His gaze met hers. "You know I don't make much working at my father's restaurant, and with my car and gasoline, well, it's taking longer than I expected."

"That's okay, Bobby." She felt bad for mentioning it now.

"I really do love ya, Donna," he assured. His car pulled up to the front of her house. Bobby leaned over and kissed her goodbye.

She opened the car door. "I love you too, Bobby."

Donna read the disappointment in Bobby's eyes before he'd driven away.

True love is not hasty. It will wait. She recalled Momma's words. If only Momma were there now. *How I miss you, Momma.* Had it only been a year since they'd lost Momma? Death was a peculiar thing, indeed. In some ways it seemed Momma had been gone for ages, but in other ways it felt like she was still here.

Two

Ben Peterson set his Bible down on the desk and removed his reading glasses. He'd heard Donna enter the house about thirty minutes ago and it seemed she was now in the kitchen working on dinner. He wondered if Pamela had made it home from school yet. As of now, he hadn't heard Daniel Landers' car in the driveway so she was most likely off doing who knows what.

It wasn't that the Landers weren't a good family. No, their boys were some of the finest in the community. They'd been in church for as long as he could remember and they were faithful members who attended just about any time the doors were open. But he'd once been a young man himself and he knew all too well of the temptations that arose when alone with a pretty girl.

He glanced at the clock on the wall of his study. Five thirty. School had been out for nearly two hours. Pamela should have been home by now. Was he overreacting? Was he just paranoid? Perhaps he needed to be stricter with his girls, but he hated to put the same burdens on them that his parents had placed on his shoulders. It seemed the rules they'd meant for his good pushed him into rebellion even more. Young people needed some freedoms too. After all, they would be adults soon and have to deal with so many more cares when they began their own families. Was there some kind of invisible line to stay behind when raising teenagers? Because, if there was, he'd really like to know where to find it. How did one know if they were being too strict or not strict enough?

The Bible had some guidelines about not provoking children to wrath and bringing them up in the nurture and admonition of the Lord, but sometimes he wished Jesus would come take his hand and show him exactly the right thing to do at each moment. Maybe then he wouldn't worry so much. He'd done much more of that since Margaret had been gone. She seemed to bring balance to their lives. How he wished she were here to talk to and share his burdens with.

"Daddy?" Donna called from his door. "Dinner's almost ready."

He smiled. "Okay, sweetheart."

"Are you alright?"

"Yes. Just thinking is all."

Donna frowned. "About Momma?"

He nodded. "Some." He arose from his chair. "Is your sister home yet?"

"No. She mentioned something about going to the library to study with Danny. I'm guessing that's where she's been. She said she'd be home about five thirty."

Ben sighed in relief. "How are you doing?"

"Me?" She shrugged. "Fine."

"Still seeing Robert Dillon?"

"Of course." She raised a brow. "Do you like him, Daddy?"

"He seems to be a good young man."

She stood on tiptoes and kissed his cheek. "Good. Let's eat now?"

The door opened and Pamela waltzed in, a smile on her face as usual. "Looks like I'm just in time." She set her books down on the coffee table. "Hi, Daddy."

"Hi, honey." Ben nodded and took his place at the head of the table. "Next time, I'd like you to be home to help your sister with dinner."

"Yes, Daddy."

They all nodded as he said the blessing, and he breathed a silent prayer of thanks for his precious daughters.

....

"Donna! Donna!" Pamela's urgent voice awakened her from a restful sleep.

"Pammy? What is it?" she said groggily.

"I'm supposed to meet Danny tonight."

"You woke me up to tell me that?" Donna turned over. "Please, just let me sleep."

"I need to borrow your car."

"No. You don't even have your license."

"Okay, then you need to take me."

"It's nine o'clock. It's too late to go out."

"Will you stop being a square and just take me?"

Exasperated, Donna rolled out of bed. "Just this one time."

Pamela wrapped her arms around Donna and kissed her cheek. "Thanks, you're the best sister ever!" she squealed.

Donna sighed and put her skirt and top back on. She looked at her sister and frowned. "Are you going to wear that mini skirt?"

"Of course, it's Danny's favorite."

"I should've known," Donna mumbled.

....

Bobby spooned some of his root beer float into his mouth. He sighed in contentment. "Man, I love these things."

Rick Landers smiled from across the booth. "Me too."

"I wish it had a little more root beer and less ice cream though," Danny spoke up.

Bobby shook his head. "Nah. It's best just how it is."

"I'd have to agree with my little brother on this one. It's sweeter than I like it." Rick frowned.

"Why don't you go ask the pretty waitress for more soda then? I'm sure she wouldn't mind serving you," Bobby challenged.

Rick shook his head.

Bobby laughed. "Danny, we've gotta find poor Rick here a girlfriend."

"I don't need a girlfriend."

"Yes, you do. You need someone to make you lighten up, enjoy life. Someone to take to the submarine races." Bobby laughed, his mind filled with memories from the last time he went with his girl.

"I'm fine right where I am," Rick insisted.

"You mean there isn't a girl out there you wish was yours?"

Rick hesitated and Bobby pounced on it. "I knew it! Who is it? Tell us!"

"Not in a million years."

"Had to do it the hard way. Now I'll just have to guess." Bobby looked to Danny. "Who could Rick have a crush on?"

Danny grinned and shrugged.

Bobby's eyes narrowed at Danny. "Do you know who it is?"

"I have my suspicions." Danny smiled.

"Like who?"

Danny glanced at his brother. "It wouldn't be fair to say."

"Danny..."

"My lips are sealed." He zipped his lips, then unzipped them to drink his float.

"Fine then. I'll guess." Bobby returned his focus to Rick. "Karen Bradshaw."

Rick tipped his head back and laughed, most likely at the thought of him and the most popular girl in school together. It was a ridiculous guess, and Bobby knew it.

"Diane Williams."

His best friend shook his head, still chuckling.

Bobby continued, bringing to mind every girl Rick would *never* date. Let's see, there was the librarian, "Barbara Copeland," the mayor's snooty daughter, "Julia Hammond," the self-proclaimed 'free spirit,' "Ann Davis." He wasn't able to finish his list as his voice dissolved into laughter. He, Rick, and Danny laughed until tears blurred their sight and their limbs were helplessly weak.

"I may just stay single forever if I don't have any other options."

"I wouldn't blame you." Bobby swiped at the moisture lingering beneath his eyes. "So who is the lucky girl you've set your sights on?"

Rick shook his head.

"Still not gonna tell me?"

"Nope."

Bobby swallowed his disappointment. Every person was entitled to their own secrets, he supposed. He sighed dramatically. "Well, how can I warn her about you if I don't know who she is?"

"Warn her about what?"

"About your unhealthy love for Parcheesi, about that one time when you ate so much popcorn you–"

Rick elbowed him. "Don't talk so loud! And besides, you're the one who dared me to eat all that popcorn."

"I didn't make you eat it."

"As good as."

Bobby laughed. "That really was funny."

"You weren't the one with corn kernels stuck in your teeth for two weeks."

"True."

Danny entered the conversation. "Speaking of popcorn, I'm meeting Pamela at the movies tonight. Are you coming with me, Rick, or are you gonna catch a ride home with Bobby?"

"I don't know." Rick shrugged. "A movie sounds good."

"Well, I don't mind if you wanna ride back with me. You know I have plenty of room." Bobby turned at the sound of the door opening. Into Mack's Diner stepped a beautiful, and very familiar, blonde. Linda, his ex-girlfriend. "Lindy," he whispered.

"What was that, Bobby?" Rick looked to see who held his attention. "Oh."

"Yeah." Bobby's gaze met its intended target and she smiled back. There had been several factors leading up to their breakup two years back. Several. Except, right now, Bobby couldn't remember any of them. But he remembered their last few dates very well. Especially last Saturday night.

"Well, we're gonna get going, Bobby."

He pulled his stare away from Linda. "What?"

Rick frowned. "I'm going with Danny to the movies. You wanna come with us?"

"Donna might be there. Sometimes, she has to chaperone me and Pam."

Bobby shook his head. "Uh, not right now. I'm gonna go talk to Lindy."

"I'm not sure that's the best idea."

"Don't worry, Lindy and I are in the past. I'm just gonna talk with her."

Three

Rick Landers sighed as the lights dimmed and the picture show began. Bobby really should have been here with him but the last he saw, Bobby and his ex-girlfriend were leaving Mack's Drive-In together in his friend's car.

Bobby had said he and Linda were in the past but, by all observances, they were very much in the present. He shook his head, lost in his thoughts. *Poor Donna. If she only knew what type of monkey business Bobby has been up to lately.* Of course, Rick couldn't and wouldn't be the one to spill the beans. It was Bobby's business and he'd leave the telling to him, no matter how he ached to tell Donna.

If he ever did decide to tell, Donna might suspect his affection for her and that might not end well. Truth was, he'd had a crush on her since middle school. He'd always been too shy to ask her out though. When Bobby and his family moved into town his sophomore year, his best friend had taken an immediate interest in Donna. Rick hadn't been worried at first since Bobby was going steady with a girl at another high school - *Linda*. But then he broke things off with her. And since Bobby was the outgoing type, he had no qualms about asking Donna out. Rick could have kicked himself for not asking Donna out when he'd had the opportunity.

Some guys had all the luck.

....

Donna's eyes attempted to adjust to the dark theater. Pamela and Danny had made their way toward the front, but she preferred to be in the back. She glanced at the chairs around and tried to locate a good spot as soon as light from the screen illuminated the auditorium. She found a nearly empty row and shuffled into a seat.

She glanced over to the moviegoer next to her and gasped. "Rick? Is that you?"

"Donna?" His brow shot up. "You're here alone?"

"No. Pammy's here with your brother." She whispered. "I had to drive her."

He nodded in understanding.

"Are *you* here alone?"

"Uh, yeah. Someone was supposed to join me but they decided to do something else instead."

"Oh." For a moment, she thought it might be Bobby then she remembered he'd called and said he had to work tonight. Had Rick been stood up by a girl? She wouldn't ask.

"Would you like some popcorn?"

She looked at his empty hands. Was he going to buy some? "Oh, no, that's alright. They charge too much for it."

"My treat." He smiled. "I'll be right back."

An usher moved to the end of their aisle and shined a flashlight in their direction. "Shh..."

Rick put a finger to his lips and Donna giggled after the usher disappeared.

"Oops," he whispered.

Donna watched Rick exit and smiled. He had always been one of the kindest boys she'd ever known. She was surprised she'd never seen him with a girlfriend. A young man like Rick would be a fine catch for some lucky girl. If she wasn't dating Bobby, she might just consider Rick Landers. Not that he'd ever ask her out.

Besides, Bobby was her one and only love. She smiled, thinking of his mention of marriage the other day. Who knew how long it would be before she became Mrs. Robert Dillon?

Rick returned a couple of minutes later with two paper bags of popcorn and two drinks. "I got you a Coke. Is that okay?"

Donna smiled. "Yes, thank you."

"I prefer vanilla Coke, but we'd have to go to Mack's for that. He's got the only soda fountain in town that I know of," he whispered.

She took a sip and closed her eyes. "Vanilla Coke is my favorite too."

He offered one of the bags of popcorn to Donna and she grabbed a handful of the buttery goodness.

"Mm...I feel like I haven't had popcorn in ages."

"It smelled so good, I couldn't resist."

A quiet settled over them and they began watching the movie. Before long, Donna felt her eyes drifting shut.

....

A smile tugged at Rick's lips as Donna's head leaned against his shoulder. Her soft snore didn't bother him one bit. He slipped his arm around her and allowed her to fully get comfortable, her head resting on his chest. The sweet smell of her shampoo didn't help dissuade his thoughts of her. Oh, man, having Donna this close felt like a dream. It almost seemed like they were on a date. Almost.

Rick mentally chastised himself for dwelling on Bobby's girl. He shouldn't even be having feelings toward her, but it was something he couldn't really help. He'd had a crush on Donna for so long, no other girl had even turned his head.

He could hardly believe Bobby would cheat on a girl, especially one as special as Donna. She was everything a guy could ever ask for in a girl – kindhearted, friendly, devoted – beautiful inside and out. Part of him wanted to share what he knew about Bobby's clandestine activities with Donna, but the other part didn't want to see her get hurt. It might be better if she never knew. Not to mention, it wasn't really his place to do the telling. It was something that should be between her and Bobby. The fact that Bobby was his best friend also weighed in on his decision not to tell. Bobby would certainly be livid if Rick squealed on him. He wasn't willing to risk losing Bobby's or Donna's friendship.

He sighed, determining that keeping his mouth shut was probably the best thing. But it killed him to know how much it would hurt Donna if she ever found out. She'd surely be devastated.

As the closing credits appeared on the screen, Rick

gently nudged Donna's shoulder. "Donna." He cleared his throat. "The movie's over."

Donna's eyes popped open and she looked around. "Oh, I fell asleep on you. I'm sorry."

"Hey, it's no problem." He grinned.

She yawned and stood up, the lights in the auditorium coming to life. "I'd better go find my sister. Thanks for the popcorn and soda, Rick."

"My pleasure." *Truly*. He stood up and stretched his legs.

Rick watched as she moved toward the front of the auditorium to find her sister. Pamela and his younger brother Danny had been dating for several months now. His brother cared deeply for Donna's sister and he could see them possibly marrying in the future. If only *he* could find someone. Perhaps it was time to take inventory of his non-existent love life and seriously start looking for a girl of his own.

....

Donna approached Pamela and her boyfriend at the front of the theater. Danny didn't seem to mind Pammy clinging to his arm. Her pleading features told Donna that she was about to ask for a favor.

"What is it? Donna sighed.

"Danny's going to take me home. Do you mind driving home by yourself?"

Donna shook her head. "Daddy wouldn't like that."

"Oh, come on, Donna! I'll be home by midnight, I promise."

Donna glanced at her watch. "It's eleven now." She doubted her sister's words held truth.

"I will," Pammy insisted.

Donna acquiesced, knowing how difficult it could be to find time to spend time with the one you loved. "Okay. But no later than midnight or I'll tell Daddy and he'll come looking for you. You'll be grounded for at least a month."

"Donna, stop trying to be Momma."

Donna frowned. "I'm not. If I was Momma, I'd be saying no."

Pamela turned to Danny. "Let's go?"

Danny nodded and smiled. "All right, if you're sure." He briefly glanced at Donna.

Pamela smiled. "I'm sure."

....

Rick stepped out of the movie house and searched for his brother's car. He could have sworn Danny had parked it in the lot to the side of the theater. *Where could it be?*

He turned to go back into the theater and find his brother. "Oh, I'm sorry!" He managed to bump right into a patron as he swung the door open. His eyes widened in surprise. "Donna?"

"I'm sorry, I should have paid more attention to where I was going."

"No, it wasn't your fault. It was mine."

She laughed. "How is it that we keep running into each other?"

He shrugged. "Oh, I don't know. Fate?"

Donna smiled.

"You haven't seen my brother, by any chance, have you?"

She nodded. "Yeah. He and my sister just left in his car."

"You're kidding." He frowned.

"Nope."

"Ah man, I can't believe Danny would leave without me!"

"Maybe he forgot you were here?"

Rick shrugged. "I don't know."

"Well, I could give you a ride. I wouldn't mind." Donna smiled. There was that kindheartedness showing through again.

"Truly?"

She nodded.

"I hate to impose."

"It's no imposition at all. Besides, I could use some company to keep me awake. Pammy pulled me out of bed to come here tonight."

"Ah, now I know why you fell asleep on me." He teased. "Are you that tired? 'Cause if you are, I could drive you home and then walk to my house. It's only a couple of blocks."

"No, I don't want you to have to walk. Why don't you drive to your house and I can drive after I drop you off?"

"That sounds like a plan."

She held the keys out to him.

....

"I'll see you in church tomorrow. Thanks for the ride." Rick waved goodbye to Donna as he closed the vehicle's door.

"It was great talking to you. I never realized we had so much in common. I thought for sure I was the only one in the world who loved Parcheesi." She laughed.

"That's the best game ever. Maybe we'll have to play sometime."

"Yeah, I'd like that. No one else ever wants to." She stuck out her best pouty lip then smiled.

"I know what you mean." His eyes shared her mirth. "Goodnight, Donna."

Donna sighed in contentment. Now that she was nearly home, she didn't feel as tired as she had earlier. Their conversation must've revived her.

A few minutes later, in her room, she moved to her closet and picked out Bobby's favorite dress to wear to church tomorrow. After church, they'd planned a picnic and she'd been looking forward to it all week.

Four

Rick waited in Bobby's driveway and tapped his steering wheel. Bobby finally emerged after twenty minutes.

"Hey, sorry to keep you waiting, man, but I had to get a shower. I overslept."

"Not a problem, but it looks like we might be late to church." He turned and looked at his friend. "Speaking of late, how long did you stay out last night?"

Bobby's brow shot up and a sly smile highlighted his features. "With Linda? Mm...I guess till about two."

Rick frowned. "Two? What did you do till two?"

"We went up to the bluff. Submarine races, you know." Bobby laughed and shook his head. "If you're asking me to kiss and tell–"

"Kiss and tell? What about Donna? I thought *she* was your girl." Rick's stomach began churning.

He waved his hand in front of his face. "What she doesn't know won't hurt her."

"Man, that's just wrong."

"Look, Linda is a fine girl. You saw how attractive she is. If you were in my shoes, you probably would have done the same thing."

"No, I wouldn't. Not if I had a girl like Donna." He looked out the window and sighed. "You planning on seeing Linda again?"

Bobby nodded. "Tonight."

"I thought you were going on a picnic with Donna today."

"I am. After church."

"And you're dropping Donna off and picking up Linda?" Rick had a difficult time keeping the incredulity out of his voice.

Bobby laughed. "Something like that."

"So, when are you breaking up with Donna?"

"Breaking up with her? She's my steady girl. I'm definitely keeping that one. I might even ask her to marry me soon."

"You're kidding."

"What's with you lately? Why are you on my case? Donna and I ain't married yet. I'm just having a little fun."

"I'm not so sure Donna would see it that way."

"Back off, man. It really isn't any of your business what I do in my love life. At least *I* have one."

Rick bit his tongue. There were so many things he wanted to say. Or do, actually. Bobby was a fool. He didn't realize what a gift he had. If *he* had a girl like Donna, he'd cherish her.

As they pulled into the church parking lot, Preacher Peterson stood nearby chatting with some of the congregants. A moment after they emerged from the car, he was offering his hand.

"Good morning, Richard. Robert." He nodded. "It looks like you made it just in time."

"Good morning, sir," Rick shook his hand and watched Bobby do the same.

"I trust you two are well on this fine day," the minister said as they walked toward the church building.

"Wonderful." Bobby smiled and looked over the preacher's shoulder. "Is Donna here?"

The minister glanced at his watch and smiled. "If I know my Donna, she's been here for twenty minutes already."

"Speaking of Donna, I'd like to have a word with you after the service if you don't mind." Bobby appeared a bit nervous.

"I trust you are treating my daughter well?"

Bobby cleared his throat. "Yes, sir."

"Very well, then. I'll see you after the service." The pastor quickly left them and made his way up to the platform.

Rick grimaced as he and Bobby took their seats. *Does Bobby plan on asking the preacher for his daughter's hand today? Unbelievable!*

They sat in the pew behind Donna and her sister Pamela because the sanctuary was packed, as it typically was Sunday mornings. On a normal Sunday, they usually arrived early and Bobby would sit next to Donna. But this wasn't a normal Sunday.

Sooner or later, someone was going to get hurt. Rick lamented the fact that it would most likely be Donna.

....

Bobby glanced over at Donna on the seat beside him and smiled. He found it difficult to keep his eyes on the road when Donna sat this close to him. She truly was a beautiful girl. It would be an honor to make her his wife. He was certain she would serve him well. Of course she would, she was the daughter of a preacher. That meant he'd never have to worry about her cheating on him and she'd be willing to forgive him for whatever transgressions he'd commit. Not that he'd purposely do anything to hurt her or that he'd ever cheat on her after they were married.

What do you think you're doing now?

He dismissed his convicting thought and mentally rehearsed his plan again. He reached across the seat and grasped Donna's hand in his own. The joy in her eyes told him that he would be met with no resistance. Nevertheless, nervousness still tortured his insides.

"Would you like to walk up on the pier before we eat our lunch?" He squeezed her hand.

"That sounds nice. The weather's beautiful today."

"There is no beauty that compares with the girl sitting next to me."

Donna shook her head. "You're silly."

"You're swell."

"You're a tease."

"You're a temptation."

She gasped.

"Don't have comeback, huh?" He chuckled. "That's because you know I'm right."

She smiled back at him.

He pulled his vehicle up to a nearby parking lot and killed the engine. "Come on. We'll leave the picnic basket and blanket here and come back for it later."

She gripped his outstretched hand after he opened her door, and she slid out. He pulled her close and lingered at her lips just a moment.

"Told you that you were a temptation." He felt the corner of his mouth lifting in a smirk.

"And what should I do about it?"

"Oh, I have some ideas."

Her eyebrow shot up. "Ideas?"

"Yeah. But it wouldn't be appropriate to discuss them in public."

She halfheartedly slapped his arm. "Robert Alexander Dillon! If my daddy heard you talking..."

"What? I didn't say anything inappropriate."

"And you weren't *thinking* about anything inappropriate either, right?"

"Well..."

She wagged her finger at him. "That's what I thought."

"Come, my love. You're thinking too much."

Donna huffed, but took his proffered hand anyway.

Bobby had trouble wiping the smile off his face.

....

Donna gazed down at the water that lapped under the pier and pondered what Bobby and her father might have been discussing after the church service this morning. Had Bobby seemed nervous on their short ride to the beach or was that her imagination? *Something* was off but she couldn't pinpoint what it was.

A warm breeze blew her hair back and she relished in the gentle sunshine. The fresh salty air had always been one of the things she loved about living near the ocean. She turned around to find Bobby sitting on one of the benches that lined the pier, his eyes intent on her.

"What?" She smiled.

He winked at her and patted the empty spot next to him. "Come, sit with me."

She did as bidden.

He took her hand in his. "Remember our earlier conversation about temptation?"

She nodded.

"Well," he swallowed, "I think I might have a remedy for that."

Why was he still on this subject? She found hiding her amusement difficult. Bobby seemed to have a one-track mind these days.

"No, I'm being totally serious." He rose from the bench and walked to the railing.

Oh no. Is he upset? Did I do something wrong?

He turned around and walked back toward her. "Donna?"

She had a difficult time deciphering his expression. "Yes?"

He suddenly dropped to his knee in front of her and held out his hand. "Will you marry me?"

Her jaw dropped. *Is he really asking this?* "Marry you?"

She felt moisture gathering in her eyes. "B-Bobby, you're asking me to marry you?"

"Yes!" Anticipation marked his lined forehead.

She looked down and now noticed there was a ring in the palm of his hand. "Really?"

He nodded.

"Okay. Yes! Yes, I'll marry you, Bobby."

"Oh, good!" He slipped the ring on her finger then clenched his heart. "For a minute there, you had me worried."

She gazed with awe at the small diamond in her ring.

"I hope you like it." Nervousness still tainted his tone.

"It's beautiful, Bobby! I love it." She threw her arms around him and kissed his cheek.

He moved her lips to his. She pulled back and frowned.

"What is it? What's wrong?"

"You didn't pay too much for the ring, did you?"

He shook his head. "Don't you go worrying about how much I spent. You do like it, don't you?"

"Oh, yes."

"Then that's all that matters." He stood up and pulled her from the bench. "I don't know about you, baby, but I'm dying for some lunch. Come on, let's go enjoy our picnic."

Donna shook her head. "Is that all you men ever think about is food?"

"Oh, no, we think about other things too. Like cars. Women. Money. Work. But, yeah, I would say that food probably does consume a good portion of our thoughts." He laughed.

"Well, I wouldn't want you to starve."

"Since my father owns a restaurant, I think it's safe to say that won't happen. But I do love your cooking. I'm sure your father will miss it when you're gone."

She nodded but an ache formed in her heart and dampened a bit of her previous excitement. What would happen to Daddy after she and Pamela moved out of the house? Without them or Momma there, he'd be all alone.

Five

Bobby determined that tonight would be the night that he ended things with Linda. It wouldn't be right to string her along now that he was officially engaged to Donna. *Donna*. He smiled. Today had gone perfectly. She was an amazing woman. There was no doubt in his mind she'd make the perfect wife for him. They hadn't discussed a date for their wedding, but he was hoping it would be soon. The sooner, the better as far as he was concerned.

....

Rick looked in his rearview mirror and watched in admiration and perhaps a smidgen of envy as his brother spoke quietly with Donna's sister in the back seat. He glanced at Donna in the passenger's seat and grimaced as she studied her engagement ring in adoration. Little did she realize her fiancé was out with another woman at this very moment. Oh, how he was tempted to say something. If he did, would she even believe him? Bobby would say he was interfering and would most likely be furious with him.

He rolled up to a stop sign and set the car in park.

"Chinese Fire Drill!" he hollered and jumped out. Donna, Pamela, and Danny followed suit and ran around the car. Danny took the wheel just as a vehicle pulled up behind them and the doors slammed shut. He and Donna now shared the back seat.

Donna laughed. "That was close."

Danny met his gaze in the rearview mirror. "You sure you don't want to come with us to Mack's?"

"Nah. I have to work early in the morning." Besides, he didn't want to be around Donna while he thought of Bobby cheating on her. He might end up saying something and that would just complicate matters even more than they already were. He'd let fate take its course.

Danny pulled the car up to their house. "Okay. Happy sleeping, big bro."

Rick stood at attention and saluted his brother goodbye.

"Thanks for the Parcheesi game," Donna called out.

"Truly my pleasure, but next time I'll beat you!" Rick laughed.

Donna shook her head and stuck her tongue out as the vehicle she was in pulled away from the curb.

....

Donna smiled as she leaned back against the seat. It was too bad Rick hadn't joined them. He was always a lot of fun. Both of the Landers boys were well-mannered, kind, and considerate and Donna briefly wondered if it had anything to do with their strict upbringing.

"Do you two want to go into the diner or just eat in the car?" Danny asked.

"Here's fine," Pammy answered for both of them.

Danny pulled up to Mack's Drive-In and flashed his lights. He glanced at Pamela and then Donna. "Do you know what you want to order?"

"I'll take a strawberry milkshake with whipped cream and a cherry!" Donna passed him a dollar bill and he pushed it back.

"I've got this." Danny smiled. "You're our chaperone, aren't you?"

"I suppose so." Donna shrugged. "Hey, since you're buying, I think I'll have a burger and fries too."

"Sure." Danny nodded.

Donna laughed. "I was kidding, Danny. But thanks. I really would only like a milkshake."

"No problem." He looked at her sister. "Pamela? Fries and a chocolate shake?"

"You know it." Pammy leaned over and kissed his cheek.

Danny sheepishly glanced into the back seat. "Not with your sister here."

"She's seen us kiss before." Pamela smiled.

Danny pointed toward the northern corner of the restaurant. "Hey, isn't that Bobby's car that just pulled up?"

Donna sat up and strained to see around the vehicles beside them. "I don't know."

Pamela looked back at her. What was that expression on her face? "Uh, Donna..."

"What?" She leaned over the seat.

Danny frowned. "Is Bobby with...? Uh..."

Donna blinked, and a jolt of fear struck through her heart like lightning.

"Why is he holding her hand?" Pammy's indignant voice screeched.

Bobby held the restaurant door open and, at that moment, pulled the young woman to his side and kissed her on the lips.

Donna shook her head. "No!" Tears pricked her eyes.

Pamela grabbed her hand. "Come on, we're going to go give him a piece of our minds!"

"No, Pammy! Let's just go home. I want to leave." Donna pulled her hand away and covered her face. It was a shame Bobby was cheating on her, but it was even worse that Pammy and Danny had to see her humiliation too.

Danny nodded. "We can do that. For sure."

The carhop skated up to their vehicle, ready to take their order.

Danny shook his head. "I'm sorry, we have to go."

The carhop chomped on her gum, nodded in confusion, and then moved on to the vehicle beside them.

Danny proceeded to put the vehicle in reverse.

"I *cannot* believe that...that jerk!" Pammy fumed. "Oh, I want to give him a talking-to he'll never forget."

Danny reached over and took Pamela's hand, most likely to calm her.

"Wow, I had no clue." Danny glanced to the back seat. "I'm sorry, Donna. You gonna be okay?"

She nodded, but it was a lie. No, she wouldn't be okay. She stared at the ring on her finger in disbelief...hurt... anger...and so many more emotions she didn't even want to think about. What was she going to do now?

There was no way she could ever trust Bobby again. How long had he been two-timing her? Who was the girl that he was with? Donna had never seen her around town. Where was she from? How long had he been seeing her? Had he been dating both of them this entire time? Had he given this other girl a ring too? Did she know that Bobby was dating her as well, or was she just as dumbstruck as Donna was?

It was all too much to think about. All she wanted to do right now was to go home, throw herself onto her bed, and cry into her pillow. She was certain there was nothing in this world that could heal this deep aching in her heart. Nothing at all.

Six

Donna sat on one of the logs around the bonfire and stared blankly into the huge flames that leapt into the sky. She barely heard the nearby waves crashing on the shore. The others in the youth group sang, but she couldn't open her mouth to do it. If she did, the tears would come again as they had all week.

Bobby had called for her twice but she refused to talk to him. Pamela had respected her wishes and didn't let on that Donna knew anything. She knew that task had been difficult for her sister. He'd told Pammy that he'd be at the bonfire tonight, but thankfully, he hadn't shown up. Yet. He was probably out with his other girlfriend.

She couldn't help the tear that slid down her cheek.

Her sister grasped her arm. "Donna, are you okay?"

"I want to go home, Pammy." She looked to her sister sitting next to her boyfriend. "You and Danny can stay. I'll walk home."

"You're sure?"

Donna nodded. Maybe a good walk would help to clear her head some.

"Okay, if you're sure."

"I am. You and Danny have fun, okay?"

Pamela nodded and eyed Donna with sympathy as she stood from the folding chair and began walking down the beach. From a distance, she could hear the group singing as their voices lifted to God.

....

"Donna? Donna, wait!" Bobby's voice called out behind her.

So, Bobby had shown up after all? She began jogging to get as far away from him as possible.

"Donna!" He caught up to her and clutched her arm, effectively stopping her.

She looked down at his hand and scowled as though he had leprosy. She thrust her arm away from his grip. "I have *nothing* to talk to you about!" She hated that he was witnessing her crying over him and hastily pushed the tears away.

"Donna, what's wrong, baby?" Oh, she hated that he played innocent. *Jerk!*

"What's wrong? You asked me to marry you, and you're asking what's wrong?"

"Donna, I don't understand you. You're not making any sense, baby. Of course, I want to marry you. I'd be a fool not to."

A fool, indeed. "I was at Mack's last Sunday night."

His brow shot up. "You were?"

She nodded. "Let me refresh your memory. You were with a pretty blonde girl."

His mien suddenly changed. "Oh, no."

"Oh, no! That's all you can say? You're sorry you got caught?" Her voice screeched.

"Donna, I am sorry!" His expression seemed sincere but she wasn't buying it. Not this time.

"I don't believe you."

"I swear that was the last time I'd planned to go out with Lindy. I would tell you that I was breaking up with her but it was never anything serious."

The nerve! "Oh, no, that kiss I saw you give her wasn't serious at all!"

"I don't love her, I love *you*."

"You, Robert Dillon, are a liar!"

"No, Donna. Please, believe me. I admit I was an idiot. Forgive me. *Please?*"

"I'm sorry. I can't. Not right now. Maybe not ever." Another tear dropped onto her shirt as she took Bobby's engagement ring off her finger.

His eyes grew wide. "No, don't do that."

"I don't want this anymore. Go give it to your precious Lindy." She tossed it at him and it fell to the sand, but she didn't regret it one bit. She took off in a sprint toward the parking lot. The sooner she got home, the sooner she could forget all about Bobby Dillon and move on with her life.

His words of desperation waned behind her. "Donna! Come back. *Please!*"

....

Donna forced the tears away as her feet pounded the sidewalk. How could Bobby propose marriage to her one minute, pledging his undying love, then...then *this*? How she'd loved Bobby. If only she could stop this helpless feeling, this anguish in her heart.

She'd been seeing Bobby now for over a year. How could he do something like this? How could he betray her? How could he just throw their relationship over the past year into the garbage?

What did this Lindy girl have that she didn't? But she knew. She'd seen her at the restaurant as she'd pressed up against Bobby. His Lindy was everything she wasn't – tall, blonde, perfect form. Unless he and Lindy had... No, she wouldn't allow her mind to go there.

Maybe she should be glad that she'd caught Bobby. Maybe God was showing her that he wasn't the one – that he would have cheated on her when they were married too. Yeah, she was probably better off without a guy like that.

What a fool she'd been not to have seen it. They would surely be the talk of the town now.

....

"Donna?"

She spun around. "Rick? I didn't realize I'd walked so far already."

He leapt off his front porch and sauntered toward her. He frowned the moment he looked into her troubled eyes. "Donna? What's wrong? Have you been crying?" He ached to reach out and offer comfort.

She brushed away another tear, as though frustrated

with her emotion, and sucked in a breath. "It's Bobby. He...he's been cheating on me."

He frowned. Of course, he'd already known for a while now. But Donna was unaware of that fact. It was an awkward situation to be in. "Danny mentioned Mack's. I'm really sorry, Donna."

"I can't believe it. He proposed to me, you know?" Another tear escaped her lashes. "How could he do that?"

"I don't know. I'd surely never cheat on a girl, especially one like you." *Oh no, did I actually say that out loud?*

"You're such a sweetheart, Rick. No, I couldn't imagine you would."

"Hey, uh. I've got some lemonade I just made, if you'd like a glass. And I've been aching to play Parcheesi again." Perhaps he could distract her for a little while and get her mind off her troubles.

"That's just because you lost to me last time."

He loved to see her smile so he egged her on. "Unless you're scared I'll beat you."

She gasped. "No way."

"You don't need to get home or anything, do you?"

"Nope. Seems I'm free all night."

What good fortune. "Great!" He nodded toward the house and she stepped in stride next to him.

....

Rick sighed as he finally slipped into bed, but sleep eluded him. He had a difficult time getting the giddy smile off his face. What a wild and wonderful and unexpected evening he and Donna had. He could hardly believe any of it – it was like a dream come true. He'd loved her for so long and just when he was certain he'd never have a chance with her, fate happened. The planets must have been perfectly aligned tonight, not that he believed in all that stuff.

He was unsure how their relationship would proceed, but he was sure of one thing. He loved Donna with everything in him and he was determined to marry her. He closed his eyes. Maybe thinking of her kisses would plunge him into a dream-filled night.

A knock on his window drew his attention outside, distracting his ecstatic thoughts. *What's Bobby doing here?* He frowned.

Oh, man. If he'd shown up just an hour before...

He lifted the window. "Bobby? Hey, man, what's up?"

Bobby crawled through the opening, something he'd done a time or two over the last couple years. Bobby sat on the edge of Rick's bed and blew out a breath. "It's Donna."

Panic began to set in. Had Bobby seen them together? *Just keep cool.*

"Donna?" His brow shot up.

Bobby held out the ring toward him. "I messed up. She gave it back."

Does Bobby have tears in his eyes?

Rick didn't know what to say. He nodded.

"She broke up with me." The anguish in his voice couldn't be squelched. "I know I deserved it."

"What about that other girl? Linda."

Bobby waved a hand in front of his face. "I never really

cared much for her. At least, not the way I do Donna."

"What are you going to do?"

"I love her. I have to get her back. I'd planned to marry her, you know. We never discussed a date or anything but I was hoping she'd want to marry right away."

Rick gulped and stared at the wall as his friend rambled on, his dreams from just moments ago dashing before his eyes. What was he going to do?

"I mean, if we could go to Vegas this weekend that would be fine with me. But I'm guessing Donna will probably want something more formal."

"I can imagine." Rick nodded, but his emotions seemed to detach. *What have I done?*

"Hey, you got all your stuff packed?" Bobby's eyes moved to a duffel bag on the floor.

"Stuff?" He blinked.

"Yeah, for basic. Didn't you say you were leaving this week? Monday?"

"I nearly forgot." His palm smacked his forehead. "It's so soon," he mumbled to himself.

"Forgot? How could you forget something like that?" Bobby's hand clasped his shoulder. "I'm really going to miss you while you're gone, man."

Oh, no! How am I going to break the news to Donna?

Seven

Donna watched the church entrance, waiting for Rick to come in for the morning service. Would he sit by her? She surmised Rick would want to make it public that they were now a couple. For a moment, she wondered what Bobby would think, then swiftly banished the thought. She refused to dwell on him. He'd thrown their love away, while Rick obviously cherished her.

Danny and his parents entered the church house, and Donna scanned the area behind them. *No Rick. Where could he be?* Doubt immediately began assailing her thoughts. Had he purposely stayed away to avoid her?

No. She shook her head. That wasn't possible. Perhaps he'd come down with the flu or something. There had to be a good reason he wasn't here. Rick rarely missed a church meeting.

Her father approached the pulpit. "Let's all stand as we sing *A Mighty Fortress Is Our God.*"

Donna rose with the rest of the congregation and joined them in song. She had to stop herself from checking the entrance every few minutes. It was becoming evident that

Rick wouldn't be attending church today. Why? Did he now regret their relationship? Surely, that wasn't the case. But, what if it was? What if the feelings of love weren't mutual? No, Rick said that he loved her. He was a good guy. The best, actually. He would never do something like that.

Never.

Donna took a deep breath to calm her nerves. She had nothing to be worried about. Absolutely nothing. She loved Rick and he loved her.

The moment church was over, Donna leapt to her feet and sought out Danny.

She did her best to sound casual, suppressing her anxious thoughts. "Where's Rick? Did he sleep in or something?"

Danny shook his head and glanced at his parents. He motioned for Donna to follow him outside.

Once they were alone, he exhaled forcefully. "Rick's gone."

Confused panic sent her heart racing. "Gone? What do you mean?"

"He left for basic training this morning."

"Basic training? You mean, for the military?"

Danny nodded. "He'll most likely be going off to Vietnam."

"What? Vietnam? Rick's a-a soldier?" She swallowed, refusing to allow tears to surface. "How come I never heard anything about this? Nobody said anything."

"It wasn't broadcast over the airwaves. Rick didn't tell anyone but me and Bobby. He didn't want our parents to find out. They're of the mindset that we shouldn't bother ourselves with Vietnam. They're very much against the war effort."

"I had no idea."

"I'm real sorry you didn't get a chance to say goodbye or get an extra game of Parcheesi in. He did leave a letter for you, though. He asked me to deliver it." Danny pulled an envelope out of his pocket. "Here."

Donna grasped the letter and slipped it into her purse. What had Rick written? "Thank you, Danny."

"Sure thing."

Donna turned and walked to her father's Studebaker, her mind in an upheaval. *Rick was gone?* How could he just leave after they'd just begun a relationship? Did he no longer love her? She refused to believe that. Yet, why had he left? Why hadn't he told her? Why hadn't he said goodbye?

....

Donna slipped her finger under the envelope's flap and earned herself a paper cut. "Ow!" She popped her finger into her mouth.

She held the folded letter close and contemplated the words Rick may have written. Finally, she opened it and read the few lines penned within.

Dear Donna,

I'm truly sorry I had to leave. I wish I'd remembered sooner and that I'd told you. I guess it's too late now. Please forgive me.

Sincerely,

Rick

P.S. I won't forget you.

Donna frowned. It seemed Rick's letter had left her with more questions than answers. Where exactly was he going? How long would he be gone? He didn't leave an address where she could reach him so there was no way to communicate.

Did he now regret their relationship? Did he regret their love?

Instead of panicking, she chose to wait. Surely, Rick would write to her again.

....

Rick stared out the window, but he saw none of the intriguing scenery that must've been passing by. He could only think of one thing. *Donna*.

I am such an idiot!

Rick had been self-deprecating since Bobby had slipped out his window the evening before. How could he speak words of devotion to Donna one moment and just leave her the next? The brief note he'd scribbled before he boarded the bus this morning would never be enough to explain away what he'd done. It could never convey the regret he was now feeling, contemplating Donna's probable reaction to his departure. He'd never been so careless in his life. Who knows how long he'd be off at war – or if he'd even return. Would Donna wait for him or would she go back to Bobby? He suspected the latter, as regret once again clamped down and sank its teeth into his heart. If he'd ever had a chance at true love, he'd just blown it. Big time.

Deep in his heart, he knew Donna wouldn't understand.

And he was certain she'd never be able to forgive him for leaving the way he did. If only he could turn back the hands of time.

Eight

Three months later...

Pamela strode up beside Donna and bumped her hip as she washed dishes at the sink.

Donna smiled. "Coming to help?"

"Not really." Pamela laughed. "But I will since you asked."

"I didn't ask. Not exactly."

Pamela shrugged and plunged her hands into the warm rinse water. "You feeling alright today? You looked terrible yesterday."

"I feel fine now."

"Daddy mentioned something about you going to the doctor."

Donna nodded. "The nurse said I have an infection and gave me some penicillin. I think it's helping."

"Oh, good. I'm glad to see you up and around again." Pamela blew out a breath. "Have you heard anything back from Rick?"

"No." Donna looked sad.

Pamela immediately regretted asking. "I'm sorry."

"It's not your fault."

"Do you think...? Well, have you thought about maybe getting back together with Bobby? You know, he hasn't seen anyone since you broke things off with him."

"No."

"So, you and Rick *are* together then?"

Donna stared at her, surprise marked her features. "I thought so. But I didn't want to say anything to anyone. In case he changed his mind, you know?"

"Does Bobby know?"

"No."

"Do you think you should tell him? I mean, if you do, he can start dating someone else."

"I'd rather he not know about me and Rick. I don't want to hurt him."

"You don't want to hurt him? What about what he did to you?" Pamela shook her head. Sometimes her sister made absolutely no sense. "If you told him about you and Rick, maybe he'd stop coming around."

"I'd rather just not say anything, okay?"

"Okay, if that's what you want."

"It is."

....

Rick brought Donna's letter to his nostrils and inhaled for a moment. He didn't know if any of her scent had lingered but he imagined it did. He closed his eyes, once again remembering the feel of her soft lips on his. How many times over the past few months had he relived those moments he'd shared with her? He reluctantly folded the letter he'd already read countless times and held it close to his chest.

"Oh, Donna," he whispered. "If you only knew how much I care about you."

"Whatcha up to, Rick?"

Rick glanced up at his friend as he approached him. "Nothin'."

Harvey grinned and plopped down next to him. "That from your girl back home?"

Rick nodded.

"I got a pretty lady waiting for me too. Virginia. Cute little thing."

"Your girlfriend?"

"Wife."

"Lucky man."

Harv smiled. "I guess I am."

Harvey had been the first to befriend him and Rick was grateful for his cheerful presence. He provided a much-wanted distraction.

"Well, I guess I'll leave you to your letter writin'. Don't forget, supper's in just a few minutes."

"You don't have to go, Harv."

"That's okay. I doubt you can write her with me around. Come find me when you're done."

Rick nodded and sighed as Harv sauntered away.

His friend was right; it was time to write back to her. He took out a piece of paper and a pen.

Dear Donna,

My heart leapt for joy when I saw your letter. I'm sorry I've taken a while to write you back. I dream about you every night and think about you all day long. Thoughts of you are what keep me going.

I can't express how much I love you and how I can't wait to see you again.

I want to marry you when I get back home. I mean it, I do.

How I wish we'd had more time together before I left. Who knows? If we'd had a month or a couple of weeks even, I'm thinking we might have been married by now.

Rick looked down at the letter and shook his head. *I can't write these words.* He couldn't do that to Donna. How could he ask her to wait until he returned? What if he died out here? What if he returned home injured and unable to provide for her? That would be selfish of him.

He sighed, ripped the letter in two, and crumbled it in his hands. If only things were different. *I'm sorry, Donna.*

Nine

Three months later...

Since lunch was awaiting them at home, Daddy had wanted to leave the church quickly. He sent Donna to find Pamela. Donna knew her younger sister would be with Danny, most likely talking by the side of the church building.

"Pamela!" she called as she neared the spot. Knowing her sister, it was best to send a warning, just in case she and her beau were kissing. She didn't doubt her sister and Danny would be getting married before too long. He hadn't asked yet, but Donna couldn't imagine he'd wait much longer now that they were both out of school.

She rounded the corner. "Pammy, Daddy said..." Her voice trailed off when she noticed the tears in her sister's eyes. Did Danny have tears in his eyes too? Had they been arguing?

Donna frowned. "Pammy, what's wrong?"

Her sister laid a hand on her arm. "Oh, Donna." She sniffed. "It's Rick."

Donna's heart froze. "What?"

Danny spoke up, swallowing hard. "We got a notice in

the mail. Rick has gone missing in action."

Missing? Donna found it hard to breathe. She stepped backwards. *How can he be missing?*

"They don't know where he is, or whether or not he's still alive."

"Oh, no." Without Rick, she had no one. *No!* Donna's thoughts screamed.

"Donna. Donna, are you okay?" Pammy squeezed her arm, drawing Donna back to the present.

She nodded, fighting her tears. "I'll be alright."

"You're sure?" The concern in her sister's eyes told her she understood her pain. But she couldn't – not really. Nobody could possibly understand.

"I'll survive." She'd grieve, for certain, but she would survive. But, would Rick? *Oh, God, please be with him.*

Donna shocked herself. When had she last prayed to God? It had been shortly after Rick had left, after she hadn't heard back from him. But she'd since moved on, hadn't she? Now, though, it all came crashing back.

"Okay. Please tell Daddy I'll be there in just a minute. I want a couple more seconds with Danny."

Donna nodded and headed back to the car, her mind and heart in an upheaval.

....

Pamela had gone upstairs to bed and Donna sat on the sofa opposite her father. Daddy read his devotions silently while Donna did her best to come to grips with the idea that Rick could be gone forever.

Daddy took off his reading glasses and studied her. "Donna."

"Yes, Daddy?"

"Have you spoken with Robert Dillon lately?"

"Bobby? No."

"I have. He's expressed more than once that he's very sorry for what he's done, Donna. For cheating on you like he did."

Donna studied her folded hands.

"Did you know that he accepted Christ as his Saviour last week?"

She glanced up in surprise. "No." She'd seen her father talking with Bobby, but she'd had no idea what it was about.

Daddy nodded. "He came to me after the service and we were able to talk for quite a while. He'd never fully grasped what Jesus had done for him before. I believe he sincerely got saved."

Why was Daddy telling her this? "That's good."

Daddy folded his reading glasses and set them down on the armrest. "Donna, have you forgiven Bobby for cheating on you?"

She nodded.

"I'm glad. He seems like a very nice young man. He loves you, Donna."

She didn't respond.

"It's been, what, about six months since you two dated?"

Donna nodded.

Daddy sighed. "Donna, I have no desire to pressure you to do something you aren't willing to do, but I believe

Bobby is truly sorry, and he wishes to earn back your heart. If you want him to leave you alone, let me know and I'll tell him. But if you're willing to give him a second chance, it would make him very happy." Daddy smiled. "And I would like to see you happy again."

Donna bowed her head. There was no way her father could know that Bobby had nothing to do with her loss of joy. There was no way she would ever tell him. What if she were to give Bobby a second chance?

Before she had held out hope that Rick would return and marry her, but with him now missing in action, that dream seemed impossible. Besides, she had no idea whether Rick even cared for her. He'd never written her back. She realized she'd been a fool to count on Rick. If he'd wanted her to wait for him, he surely would have asked her to.

Would it really be so bad if she married Bobby?

"Would you be willing to give Bobby another chance?" Daddy met her gaze.

Donna attempted a slight smile and nodded.

....

Bobby held his hand out to Donna and she offered hers. The smile he sent her was nearly timid. There was no doubt the events that had transpired over the past year changed Bobby.

Donna rested her head on his shoulder as they stared out at the ocean.

"Remember when you first took me to see the submarine races?"

Bobby shook with laughter. "How could I forget?"

Donna couldn't help but grin at the memory. "I had never heard of it before and I was excited to go. I thought it'd be like boat racing."

"Except that submarines stay underwater." Bobby chuckled.

"I figured that out eventually. After staring at the empty water for about five minutes."

"You couldn't figure out why I kept trying to cuddle when we came to see the race." Bobby's eyes danced in merriment. "And then I explained what submarine races were."

Donna covered her face with her right hand. "I was so embarrassed."

Bobby reached for her hand and pulled it away from her face. His eyes met hers. "It just made you all the more sweet to me." He leaned in and touched his lips to hers, his hesitance new.

Donna returned his kiss but found Bobby pulling back before it could deepen.

"Donna, I-I want to do this right. I messed up big time before and I don't want to do that again. I'm willing to be patient. I'm willing to wait for you. We can go as fast or as slow as you want to. I'm ready to marry you, Donna, but you hold the reins. This time, I promise to treat you with the respect you deserve."

Tears rushed to Donna's eyes and began the journey down her cheeks. "Thank you," she managed to whisper. She returned her head to Bobby's shoulder, marveling in the love that – despite what Bobby said – she didn't deserve.

....

Summer 1969...

"Okay, Donna, it's almost time! I can hear the music starting." Pammy beamed at her.

"How do I look?"

"Absolutely beautiful." Pamela gave her a quick hug. "I can't believe you're getting married."

"You can't believe I'm getting married? How about yourself? You'll be in my shoes before too long." Donna looked at her sister's left hand pointedly.

Pammy admired her ring. "I know, I can't wait! Danny is easily the best man in the world."

"Hey, now. What about me?" Daddy joined them, a smile on his face.

"Well, you're pretty swell yourself, Daddy. But, no offense, I certainly don't want to marry you."

Daddy laughed. "No offense taken."

The music changed and Pammy's eyes widened. "That's our cue!" She turned as the double doors opened and stepped out into the church aisle.

Daddy placed Donna's hand on his arm. "Are you ready?" he murmured.

She nodded. *Ready as I'll ever be.*

Donna plastered a smile on her face as she and her father began their walk up the aisle. Bobby grinned at her from his position on stage and her heart warmed. In the months since their breakup, Bobby had proven again and again that he was a different man, that he would never make the same mistake again. For that, Donna was eternally grateful. With his amorous devotion, Bobby had regained her love. And now, a year since he had first proposed, she and Bobby were actually getting married. For better or worse. Till death parted them.

Daddy released her arm when they reached the stage and stood before the congregation. "Today is a day of rejoicing as we join Donna Peterson and Robert Dillon in holy matrimony. Please be seated."

So much had occurred since Donna had first agreed to marry Bobby. A lot of fear, pain, and regret. If she had been granted the opportunity to erase a year of her life, it would have been the past year. Donna prayed she was a stronger person for the many trials she had experienced. She hoped to face her new life with Bobby, free of past wrongs and mistakes. Lord willing, their future would shine brighter than their past ever had.

"Donna Marie Peterson, do you take this man, Robert Alexander Dillon, to be your lawfully wedded husband in the sight of God and these witnesses?"

Donna nodded and met the gaze of her soon-to-be husband. The tears of joy sparkling in his eyes spoke volumes. "I do."

....

Three months later...

A smile lit Donna's face as Bobby entered the house and shucked his shoes. He approached the kitchen and came up behind Donna. He nuzzled her neck, wrapping his arms around her.

"Good day at the restaurant?"

"Mm...hm."

Donna leaned back in Bobby's strength, ignoring dinner on the stove.

"Does being manager suit your liking?"

Bobby nodded. "I like it. I'm grateful Pops left me the position."

"Did he look over your shoulder all day?"

"Not today. He stopped by for a few minutes and that's all. I think he's getting used to the idea that I don't need his help anymore."

"I'm sure it's difficult for him to see you as a grown man, not just his son."

"I agree." Bobby peeked into the oven. "Meatloaf?"

"And mashed potatoes and gravy and steamed broccoli." Donna checked the veggies.

"Have I told you lately that I love you?" Bobby grinned at his reference to the song and kissed her.

Donna pretended to consider his words. "I think so. Though I won't complain if you say it again."

Bobby placed his hands on the counter behind her, guarding all escape routes. Not like Donna would ever want to escape him. "Donna, I love you."

She closed her eyes in anticipation of his kiss. Bobby's hand brushed past her waist and her eyes flew open in time to see him pop a piece of broccoli into his mouth.

"Hey!" She smacked his arm.

He grinned unrepentantly as he chewed his mouthful. "It's really good."

"Flattery will get you nowhere, troublemaker." She huffed in mock frustration.

"Regardless, it tastes delicious." Bobby eyed the pot and Donna blocked his view.

"You're supposed to be kissing me, not sampling dinner."

"Aren't they sort of the same thing?"

Donna planted her hands on her hips and quirked a brow, doing her best to appear unamused. "Just kiss me."

Bobby smiled. "Yes, ma'am." He took her in his arms and this time managed to meet her waiting lips with his. Her hands left her waist to find the back of his neck as he drew her nearer.

One very satisfying kiss later, Donna used every inch of her willpower to release her husband and return to the stove. "Wanna help me set the table?"

He nodded. "Your wish is my command."

They set everything on the table and sat down. Bobby prayed over the meal before they began to eat.

Bobby's gaze turned serious. "So how are you feeling? Has your stomach been acting up again?"

"Not much today. I went to the doctor's to see if they could figure out what it was."

Bobby looked up from his plate. "And?"

Donna set down her fork and smiled. "The doctor confirmed my suspicions."

"Which were?" Bobby leaned forward expectantly.

"I've been eating too many sweets."

Bobby reclined back in his chair. "Oh."

Donna laughed. "I'm joking."

"What *did* the doctor say?"

"We're expecting a baby!"

"You are? That's wonderful!" A beaming smile took over Bobby's face. He glanced down at her flat stomach. "When will the baby be born?"

She chuckled at his enthusiasm. Enthusiasm she attempted to catch. But it was hard to consider giving birth to a child when... She brought her train of thought to an immediate halt. She couldn't give in to the sadness now, not when Bobby expected her to be as excited as he was, as excited as she *should* be. "I'm only six weeks along, honey. So, it'll be quite a while."

"What will we name him? Or her. It."

Donna shrugged. "Whatever we decide."

"I like Robert Jr. for a boy." Bobby grinned.

"And Margaret for a girl."

"After your mother?"

Donna nodded.

"I like it." Bobby nodded once, then touched a hand to her stomach. "Hello, Robert or Maggie. This is your daddy."

Donna placed her hand atop his. "And this is your momma."

Bobby leaned down slightly, speaking to her belly. "You be sure to stay safe in there and grow up good and strong, okay?"

"We love you," Donna added.

"Yes, we do." Bobby looked up at Donna. "What if there's a Robert and a Maggie in there?"

"Twins?"

He nodded.

"I think twins have to be a genetic thing. I don't know of any twins in my family."

"I don't have any in my family either." Bobby shrugged.

"One baby will be just fine."

"For now. Little Robert or Maggie will need someone to play with. We don't want them to be lonely."

Donna smiled. "We sure don't."

Ten

June 1970...

Bobby bounced through the door of his and Donna's house with a smile plastered on his lips. Oh, how he loved this time of day – coming home to his beautiful wife, eating the delicious meal she'd prepared, enjoying her company for the rest of the evening, and then relaxing in her arms. Before too long, they'd have a little one to occupy their time as well. He was a blessed man.

He prayed Donna's pregnancy would go well this time around. When their firstborn baby entered the world stillborn, he didn't think there was anything more difficult that a parent could go through. Although he still grieved the loss of Robert Jr, just three months prior, he realized he truly was a blessed man in spite of their misfortune. He still had Donna.

The delicious aroma of roast beef, potatoes, and carrots wafted through the air and lured him to the kitchen. *Where is Donna?* He thought it strange that she wasn't at the door, ready to greet him with a kiss. That had been his usual homecoming treat, which he enjoyed immensely. Perhaps she was in the bedroom changing.

"Donna?" He called out but received no response.

A groan down the hall caused his spine hairs to stand on end. He rushed toward the bathroom and knocked on the door.

Bobby began to panic. "Donna, are you okay?"

"It's the baby, I think." Another groan.

A familiar sense of terror laced his heart. "Will you open the door?"

"I can't!"

Bobby ran to the kitchen and retrieved the ice pick from the utensil drawer. "Okay, I'm coming in." He burst through the door to find his wife on the floor in the fetal position. "Donna!"

He scooped her up into his arms and rushed her to their bedroom, where he gently set her on the bed. "Baby, what's wrong? How can I help you?"

Donna moaned.

"Just stay there. I'm calling the doctor." He rushed from the room.

....

Bobby clenched the steering wheel and glanced at the rearview mirror. Donna curled forward, holding her abdomen with shaky hands. Her half groans, half sobs tore at his heart. Desperation turned his foot to lead as he raced to the hospital. He tried to pray, but his panicked mind refused to form sentences.

Oh, God. Please.

After the loss of their first baby, Bobby wasn't certain he

could handle more grief. He and Donna had prayed and prepared for Robert Jr. for months. They'd settled on a name, they'd painted and furnished the nursery. When he'd been born lifeless, their hopes and dreams had been crushed. Somehow, Bobby thought it had been his fault.

Donna had been more hesitant to get excited about the baby. She'd seemed almost paranoid and Bobby had done his best to shake her out of whatever haze she was in. He'd presented his most optimistic front, he'd gone above and beyond in his preparations for the baby, and had slowly helped Donna gain her confidence and excitement. But when they saw their stillborn child and Donna sobbed into his arms at night, it had seemed like his fault. Perhaps if he hadn't pushed so hard, his wife wouldn't have grieved so deeply.

Bobby promised God that he wouldn't do the same thing again and prayed all the more for a healthy child. When Donna discovered she was pregnant again, they were both glad, but also cautious. There was no doubt that they loved their unborn baby, but they held their concerns higher than their hopes, all the while praying for the best.

And now this.

Dear Jesus, be with our baby. Please, please be with our baby.

....

"Mr. Dillon, may I have a word with you?"

Bobby turned at the doctor's voice and nodded. He looked back at Donna, who appeared to be sleeping, and joined the doctor behind the curtain.

Bobby stepped near the doctor and spoke in a low tone so as not to awaken Donna. She needed her rest after their latest ordeal. "What is it, Dr. Andrews?"

"I don't really know how to say this, but I think it needs to be mentioned." He rubbed his chin. "I think I've been able to determine the cause of your wife's troubles."

"Go on," Bobby urged, noticing the doctor's slight hesitation.

"She has an unusual amount of scar tissue that I'm guessing is from a..." – His brow shot up. – "...former surgery?"

Bobby frowned. Was he supposed to know what the doctor meant by that? "As far as I know, she has never had any surgeries. Just, you know, from the last time she lost the baby."

"The scar tissue was present prior to Donna's previous miscarriage."

"I'm afraid I'm not understanding your meaning, Doctor."

"Has Donna ever had an abortion?"

"An abortion? I'm not sure I even know what that is."

"It's when a woman goes to a doctor to have an unborn child removed – a *live* unborn child."

"What do you mean by removed?"

"Sometimes, Bobby, when a young woman gets pregnant before she's married, she will choose to have a doctor dispose of the child inside her womb."

Bobby's eyes widened. "You mean, kill it?" He couldn't imagine such a thing. *What kind of person would do that?* "But that's murder. It's wrong."

The doctor nodded. "Yes, and against the law." He frowned. "Although there are those among us who'd like to change that."

"I pray that never happens."

"Me too, son."

Bobby shook his head. "I can assure you, Doctor, that my Donna wouldn't ever do something like that. Her father is a minister. And we waited until we were married, so there's no chance of that."

The doctor nodded. "I see. Well then, I'm glad to hear it."

Bobby determined he wouldn't say anything to Donna about this. She'd already been so upset that they'd lost their babies. She didn't need to know that there were others out there that would terminate their baby's life on purpose. The thought still caused his skin to crawl.

Eleven

Donna overheard every word the doctor and Bobby spoke and tears pricked her eyes. Could *she* be the reason they'd lost this one and little Robert Jr.? No, it couldn't be true. It just couldn't. She closed her eyes and recalled something she'd desperately tried to forget over the past few years. Yet, no matter how many times she tried, it never went away...

Summer 1968

Rick folded the board to the Parcheesi game and tucked it into its box. He glanced at Donna's hand once again. "I noticed you're not wearing your ring." It seemed like more of a question than a statement.

She looked down at her finger and a fresh wave of tears assaulted her. "No, I gave it back."

He leaned against the divan and moved his focus to the beautiful young woman at his side. How he longed to comfort her. What he wouldn't give for a chance with her. Bobby had to be out of his mind. "Donna, Bobby really isn't that bad of a guy."

"Rick, please. Don't. I know he's your best friend but it's

different with us. He..." She brought a tissue to her face and dried the wetness. "We've been going steady for nearly a year. He just threw that all away – like I was garbage. Like I didn't even matter. Our relationship meant nothing to him."

"I truly am sorry." He blew out a breath.

"I don't want to talk about Bobby right now. I'm so frustrated with him."

He moved to touch her hand then thought better of it. "Is there something I can do? I'd like to help you, Donna. Truly."

"Rick, how is it that you don't have a steady girl?"

Because I'm in love with you. He shrugged. "I don't know. I just haven't found the right girl, I suppose."

"You know, Rick, I think you're the sweetest guy I've ever known. If Bobby and I hadn't..." She shook her head.

Could this be his opportunity to reveal his true feelings for her? If he didn't take a chance he'd never know if they could ever have something more. It was now or never. "Donna?" He began gently. "I...I've always cared for you."

Her gaze met his and she reached over and stroked his hand. "I consider that an honor, Rick."

"Is it possible...I mean, do you think we could...?" Could he really ask Bobby's girl to go out? Should he just keep his thoughts to himself? But it was too late.

She lifted a brow. "Date?"

He nodded with a confidence he did not feel.

She moved her hand to intertwine their fingers. "I'd love to."

"Really? You would?"

She moved closer and he felt an overwhelming desire to draw her into his arms and kiss her breathless. But he wouldn't. He'd let her make the first move.

"Yes, I most definitely would." This time she did meet his lips with hers.

Rick pulled Donna closer and deepened the kiss. He thought she might end it when she pulled back for a breath, but instead she wove her fingers through the hair at the nape of his neck. His hands caressed her back and the feel of her form against him had his heart racing like never before. With each breath, their kisses intensified until he admitted to himself they should probably stop, although he had no desire to. He would allow Donna to hold the reins. He was at her mercy.

....

Donna's eyes flew open and she remembered where she was. Rick's strong arms held her close to his chest and she snuggled against him. His soft snore suddenly ceased and his warm breath nuzzled her neck, sending a shiver of delight through her.

"What time is it?" he mumbled.

She looked at the clock on his nightstand but had trouble deciphering it through the dim moonlight filtering through the curtains. *It's almost midnight?* "Oh, no. I should get home."

He leaned in and met her lips. The spark of passion from just hours before threatened to reignite. He pulled back and caressed her face. "Yes, you should. But I wish you could stay here in my arms forever."

Rick's sweet words temporarily alleviated the guilt that had begun seeping into her soul and soothed some of her anxiety. She scanned Rick's room and her cheeks warmed as she realized she'd have to get out of Rick's bed and locate her clothes.

"I'll walk you home," Rick whispered. He quickly found his jeans and threw his Pendleton on. "We'll need to be quiet. I think my folks are probably sleeping."

"Oh, no."

"Shh...it's alright. We just need to keep quiet. They're down the hall. We'll just slip out through my window, okay?"

She nodded as she finished buttoning her dress and found her shoes.

The walk home had been mostly quiet. She supposed they were both deep in thought. As they neared her house, they stopped at the end of the block.

"I should probably walk the rest of the way alone," she suggested.

"You're probably right." He pulled her close and kissed her. "Donna, I love you."

"I love you too, Rick."

He lifted her chin and studied her eyes. "I know what we did was wrong, but I can't say I regret it."

"You don't?"

"How can I? Donna, you are amazing. You're everything any guy could want." He frowned. "*You* don't regret it, do you?"

"We sinned, Rick." She shook her head. "You...you were my first. Bobby and I had never—"

"I know." His thumb brushed her cheek. "And I'm truly honored."

"My daddy, he's going to..." She began to tremble and he pulled her close.

"Shh...your father doesn't need to know. Nobody will know but us, okay?"

She nodded then looked into his eyes once more. "I don't regret loving you."

"Nor I, you." He kissed the top of her head. "Goodnight, Donna. I'll wait here until you wave to me from your window."

"Goodbye, Rick."

....

Donna turned her hymnal to the designated page number. Suddenly, she felt like a hypocrite, to be singing and worshipping God when she had so blatantly disobeyed Him just hours ago. The small cross adorning the pulpit seemed to condemn her, calling her out on her sin. What if they all knew? What would Daddy say? What would Pammy think?

And Bobby... If Bobby knew, he would call her ten times a hypocrite. To think of how she had refused his attempts at intimacy, then had turned around and done the unthinkable with his best friend. His cheating on her paled in comparison to what she and Rick had done.

She could never tell a soul.

By his fervent words of love last night, she imagined he would want to be near her. Why wasn't he in church this morning? Did he feel the same guilt and shame she was now feeling? Had he needed more sleep after their late night together and decided to sleep in?

The service flew by but Donna didn't hear a word. The memories of Rick's touch, his whispered words of love, and his passionate kisses blocked all other sound and thought.

....

Rick couldn't be gone! After all they'd said and done...

"Donna!"

Her spine stiffened at the sound of Bobby's voice, of his footsteps nearing her. She continued striding to her father's vehicle.

"Donna, please. I'm sorry. I'm really sorry. I should never have cheated on you."

She refused to look at him, to pause, to acknowledge his presence in any way.

Bobby stepped in front of her, forcing her to stop. "Babe, look at me."

Reluctantly, she did. She could see the pain in his eyes, the regret. She realized that he was truly sorry, but how could she take him back now? After what she'd done, she should be the one apologizing, begging for forgiveness. And if Rick really was gone for good... Please, God let it not be so.

"I'm sorry. I was an idiot, a jerk. Please forgive me? I'd get down on my knees and beg if it would change your mind."

Donna walked around him and opened the door to Daddy's car. She slid in and closed the door.

Bobby pressed his hands to the window. "Donna..." His voice, though muffled, could still be heard through the glass barrier. He sighed. "Is what I did that unforgivable?"

Tears welled in Donna's eyes and she turned her face away from the window. "No," she whispered, "But what I've done is."

Oh, Rick! If only you hadn't gone.

Twelve

Pamela sailed into Donna's room without knocking. "Hey, Donna. You feeling any better today?"

Donna shrugged. "Not really."

"Well, I have something that will make your day better."

Donna suddenly noticed her little sister holding something behind her back. Had Rick written to her? She sat up in anticipation. "What is it?"

"Chocolate!" She whipped a yellow package out and dropped it into Donna's lap.

Her stomach dropped and she sagged back against her pillow. No letter. Donna fought to control her disappointment as her sister jabbered on.

"They're the semi-sweet kind that you like, though how you can eat them is beyond me. Chocolate is supposed to be candy. That stuff's not even all that sweet." Pam paused and studied Donna for a second. "Well, aren't you gonna eat some?"

Donna nodded and opened the package. She poured a small helping of chips into her palm and popped them into her mouth, smiling in an attempt to appease her sister.

"Oh, and you won't believe what I heard at Fowler's."

Donna had no interest in Pam's words. Fowler's Five and Dime was more of a meeting hall for town gossips than a grocery store.

"–pregnant–"

Donna's insides froze. "What?"

Pamela nodded, her eyes wide. "I know, I was so shocked! I never would have expected it of Peggy. Karen Bradshaw, maybe, but Peggy was always so, I don't know, pure? To think that she's pregnant out of wedlock..."

"You should have heard what Mrs. Hammond was saying about her. No, never mind, you shouldn't. Nobody should. It's hard to believe she's the mayor's wife and head of the gossip mill. One would think her occupations would conflict at some point."

Donna could only imagine the words. Harlot. Tramp. Tart. Sinner. An embarrassment. Shame to her family, to the community. If she truly was carrying Rick's child, like she suspected, those words would soon be spoken about her. That had to be the reason for her sickness, there was no other explanation.

"Mrs. Hammond was telling everyone to shun her, to refuse to talk to her, to even look at her. 'We shouldn't sully ourselves with sinners like her.' She actually said that. I wanted to slap her so badly, but I managed to hold it in. Instead, I reminded her that we're all sinners, including her. And you know what she did? She sniffed and said, 'I see we can expect you to follow her immoral ways.' I tell you, it took everything in me not to slap the woman then and there.

Imagine what she'd say then." Pammy snorted.

"Everyone seems to think Peggy's damned to hell because she's pregnant. Honestly, I don't think it's that big a deal. I mean, I know it's a sin, but she and Mike are getting married. And Mrs. Hammond forgets what it's like to be young and in love. It's hard not to get carried away." Pamela looked to Donna, as though suddenly realizing she wasn't just talking to herself.

"Don't worry. Danny and I haven't done anything–" Pink stained her cheeks and halted her words. "Well, we haven't gone that far. We both know Daddy would kill me if we did." She laughed.

Her sister's careless words seemed like arrows piercing Donna's heart.

If Daddy were to ever find out...

....

Donna checked the mail again. Still no letter back from Rick. She'd been able to acquire his field address from Danny and sent him a note asking him to contact her on an important matter. She'd been cryptic, so as not to give away any private information, but she hoped Rick understood the underlying message – she *needed* to talk to him.

After not hearing from Rick these last couple months, Donna finally came to the realization that Rick was no longer interested in their relationship – he was through with her. *Did he just sweet talk me so he could have something to brag about to his military buddies?* She held back the tears for as long as possible. She would have refused to cry but her tear ducts disobeyed. *Rick used me!* Just the thought made her want to vomit.

She had been so, so wrong about him. How could he pledge his love and then skip town? And now, knowing what she was pretty sure to be true – that she was carrying Rick's baby – what on earth was she supposed to do about it? She had no way to get a hold of him. And even though she'd written him a letter, well, this was news that should only be uttered in person. What if the letter found its way into the wrong hands? Not that it would matter now. Soon, the whole town would be branding the preacher's daughter a harlot.

How could she let Daddy go through that? How could she heap this shame upon him after he'd been nothing but kind and good to her? He was still grieving the loss of Momma. She was unsure if he could bear this hardship too. He'd blame himself for not being a good father, which was certainly not true. And what about the church? He could lose his job, couldn't he? If nothing else, he'd probably lose most of his congregation.

If only she could go away. If she could go away then Daddy wouldn't have to know about the baby. But then what would she do? How would she support herself? She couldn't work and keep a baby.

She broke down in tears once again. There were no easy answers.

Thirteen

Donna slid off the examining table.

"Well, dear. It looks like you're about ten weeks along." The older woman's gravelly voice evidenced years of cigarette smoking.

"You mean, I-I'm pregnant?"

The nurse examined Donna's left hand, where a ring would usually be worn with pride. "I'm afraid so."

Donna couldn't help her tears. She'd suspected, but up until now it had just been a suspicion.

The nurse patted her hand.

"I don't know what I'm going to do. My father..."

The nurse snapped her fingers together. "That's who you are! You're the preacher's daughter, aren't you?"

Donna looked at her in horror. She'd never seen this woman in her life, yet she knew who she was? Oh, no. This was not good.

"You're not married, are you, honey?"

Donna shook her head in shame. She bit her lip to keep it from trembling.

"Where's the baby's father? Will he marry you?"

"No. He's off at war. He doesn't even know. I'd hoped –"

"Those poor boys out there. Half of 'em are returning home in body bags." The nurse's eyes widened when Donna gasped. "I'm sorry, dear, but this whole war thing just does not sit well with me. Seems to me we should be minding our own business."

"I haven't heard from him since he left." She wiped away a tear.

"That's not a good sign."

"I know."

"You know, I hate to say it, but there's a good chance your baby's father may not even return. How do you plan to care for this child on your own?"

"I don't know."

"I don't often share this, but your situation is unique. My husband is a retired doctor. He occasionally does work on the side."

Donna frowned, not understanding the woman's meaning. "I'm sorry. I don't–"

"He could take care of your problem and no one would ever know. Of course, he does charge something."

"I don't quite understand."

"He can make you unpregnant. He'd remove the tissue inside."

Donna's eyes enlarged. "I didn't even know that...what... how?" She'd never heard of such a thing.

"Surgery." The nurse turned to the counter nonchalantly. "If you're interested, I'll need to inform him this week. These things need to be taken care of as soon as possible. The longer we wait, the more difficult it gets. And before long, you'll start showing and everyone will know."

"I-I'll do it."

The nurse turned back to her and nodded. "I think you've made a good decision." She scribbled something on the back of a piece of paper. "Here is the address. Be there this Friday at ten in the morning and bring a hundred dollars with you."

"A hundred dollars?" Where would she get that kind of money?

"That's his fee. Surgery is expensive, my dear." The nurse turned to walk out the door. "By the way, this will be our little secret."

Donna nodded in understanding. Good, she didn't have to worry about the nurse telling anyone.

Although Donna felt some relief, anxiety still trembled in her bones.

....

Donna managed to find the hundred dollars needed. Daddy had always kept a ceramic jar in his bookcase with emergency money in it. He'd told Donna about it after Momma died but she doubted Pammy knew of its contents. Hopefully, she'd be able to replace it before Daddy noticed that some of it was missing. If he ever found out what she planned to use it for...

She sighed heavily and attempted to dispel any negative thoughts. She should be relieved, shouldn't she? After today, she could forget about the mess she and Rick had gotten themselves into and move on with her life. Why, then, did she feel like she was making a mistake?

She knew. It was the voice inside warning her not to go through with it.

But she had to.

If only she could have talked to Rick. If only he would have stayed. They could have married right away and no one would have known. Of course, people might have suspected but at least they would be married.

But Rick wasn't there and she had no way to contact him. And like the nurse said, who even knew if he would return home alive? The thought saddened Donna. She knew she'd fallen in love with Rick. She wouldn't have given herself to him if she hadn't. He seemed like such a good, good man that had truly been in love with her too. She couldn't imagine him ever doing anything to hurt anyone. Yet, she was here carrying his offspring and he was off at war. Maybe she'd been wrong.

....

Donna took a deep breath as she approached the front door of Rick's parents' home and knocked. She had to at least attempt to contact Rick again. Perhaps his folks knew a way.

"Donna?" Mrs. Landers smiled. "What brings you by here today? I hope Preacher Peterson is doing well."

"Yes, ma'am. My father's fine." Donna mentally chided herself for fidgeting. "I'm wondering if you might have a way to contact Rick. Did he leave a phone number?" Please say yes.

"I believe Danny received a letter from Ricky the other day. He said to tell you and Bobby hello, I believe." Rick's mother forced a smile. "But no, I'm sorry, dear. We have no way to contact him by telephone. Those boys are fighting out there and..." Her voice trailed off and Donna noticed tears in her eyes.

"I'm sure you miss him, Mrs. Landers."

"Yes, we miss Ricky very much. I never thought one of my boys would be out there fighting on the other side of the world."

Donna didn't really know what to say, but she had to go soon if she was going to make her appointment.

Oh, Rick. How I wish you hadn't left!

Fourteen

Donna's heart felt like it beat a thousand miles per minute as she pulled up to the address the nurse had written down. Was she at the right place? She surveyed the mobile home situated at the end of a long secluded driveway. It didn't seem too run-down or decrepit but it definitely was not what she'd suspected. Somehow, she thought a surgery would take place in a medical facility.

Her unease grew as she walked up the wooden steps and knocked.

The door opened after a moment and the nurse from the doctor's office appeared. Donna didn't know if this calmed her more or made her more cautious. Would this woman be assisting the surgery?

"Did you bring the money?" The nurse's eyebrow rose and she held out her hand.

"Yes." Donna swallowed. She pulled the bills from her wallet and handed them to the woman.

"Very good. Come on in." The nurse took one of the bills and stuffed it into her own purse, then handed the other bills to an older, hardened looking gentleman. "This is the one," she told him.

The man nodded.

The nurse handed her what looked like an old hospital gown. "There's no paperwork or anything to sign. Just go into the bathroom there and change into this gown."

Donna nodded and quietly obeyed. Until now, she hadn't noticed the thick cigarette stench of the trailer. It almost caused her to vomit. She squeezed her eyes closed before exiting the restroom.

The man pulled back a curtain, but said nothing to her.

"Just sit in this chair here and put your legs here as you did in the doctor's office." The nurse explained.

Donna did as told.

The next hour was something she didn't think she could ever forget.

....

Even now, hours later, the sound of the suction machine haunted her. She could still recall the excruciating pain of the procedure itself. And then, the baby. As soon as she saw it, she'd gasped and nurse hastily moved the jar out of sight. She'd felt betrayed. Hadn't the nurse said the doctor would just be removing tissue? Why, then, did a tiny perfectly-formed hand end up in the mix of 'tissue'? The thought that it was already a baby, a sacred human being, at that early stage grieved her heart. What had she done?

Just the thought of it caused her stomach to roil. She ran to the restroom.

Several moments later, she locked the door to her room and sank down into her bed and sobbed like she never had before. *Oh God, what have I done? What have I done?*

It was something she'd never get over all her days. Never. And she couldn't ever tell a soul.

....

Donna opened the small gate at the entrance to the cemetery just beyond the church their family had attended since before her birth. She'd needed to talk to Momma for so long now. She'd double checked to be sure Daddy's car wasn't present. The last thing she wanted was for Daddy to see her out here crying. He would think she was grieving over Momma, and she didn't want to bring sadness to Daddy's eyes again.

But she wasn't grieving for Momma this time.

She walked to the simple marked gravestone and reread the words she'd already memorized, "Margaret June Peterson, beloved wife of Benjamin James Peterson, daughter of Alvin and June Stark, mother of Donna and Pamela, Born 1930 – Died 1967."

She sat down next to the headstone and wished with all her heart things could be different. "Oh, Momma, how I miss you!" She brushed away a tear. "I'm sorry. I'm so sorry I disappointed you. I know this isn't what you wanted from your daughters, but I messed up, Momma. I have failed you and Daddy and God and everybody else. I hate what I've become.

"Please tell God I'm sorry. And my baby...Momma, if she's there, please tell her that I was so wrong to do what I did. Tell her that I love her so so much and I miss her. If I could go back and change it, I would. I wouldn't care about what people would have said about me. I wouldn't care about any of it. I would just be happy that I have my baby. But I don't think I can ever be happy again now. When I made that decision to end her life, my joy seemed to disappear. It was as though my life ended too.

"And Rick, her daddy. I think you remember him, Momma. He's one of the Landers boys. Well, he doesn't even know. No one knows, and I'm too ashamed to admit that I did such a wretched, awful thing."

Donna sat there for a few more moments until she'd said her piece.

Fifteen

"Thanks for coming over, you two. I know I had a blast." Pammy grinned from her perch in Danny's lap.

"Thank you for having us, sis," Donna responded. "I wonder how Daddy's holding up."

Pamela laughed. "He's probably being coerced into telling Becky the story of Esther for the hundredth time. She loves that one."

A smile warmed Donna's heart at the thought of her father holding his *second* oldest granddaughter in his lap as he told her all about the Persian queen and how she rescued her people, with God's help, of course.

"Wasn't that one always your favorite growing up?"

Pammy nodded. "I always liked the idea of being queen, and the fact that Esther saved the day helped too."

Danny spoke up. "I don't know about saving the day, but you're the queen of *this* castle."

Pamela pressed a hand to her husband's cheek. "And you're the king." She kissed him.

Bobby reached for Donna's hand and wove his fingers

through hers. She smiled at her husband and rested her head on his shoulder.

What would she do without Bobby? Through all the trials she had faced, he had been her anchor, her rock. True, for a time she had lost her trust in him, but he had done everything possible to earn it back. And he had. Without Bobby beside her, Donna didn't think she could have handled the death of their first baby. And though it had been nearly two months since the loss of their second child, Donna knew her heart was beginning to heal. Bobby's strength buoyed her faith and helped her continue on, helped her learn to manage her crushing grief and find tiny joys in every day.

Donna looked away from Bobby to find her sister studying her.

"I'm happy to see you smile, Donna. How are you guys holding up?"

The room took on a somber tone as they all recalled the babies Donna and Bobby had lost.

"We're doing alright, for the most part," Bobby spoke, squeezing her hand. She met his gaze and he sent her a little smile. "Just keep going day by day, praying that God will continue to heal."

Donna nodded in agreement.

"I'm glad." Pamela looked at Danny questioningly, as though requesting permission to do something. Danny nodded and Pamela turned back to them. "Danny and I have some good news." She beamed. "We're expecting!"

"Really?" Donna stood at the same time her sister did

and enveloped her in an embrace. "Congratulations!" She gave Danny a hug as Bobby offered Pamela congratulations. "That's wonderful." Donna stepped back to Bobby's side and he put an arm around her waist.

"Thanks. We're pretty excited." Pamela grinned up at Danny, whose returning smile reflected just how much he loved her.

Donna almost felt like an intruder in the middle of their happy glow. She wondered if she and Bobby would ever experience that joy again.

....

She'd received her answer today. The doctor's words played in her mind for what seemed the hundredth time since she and Bobby left his office just twenty minutes ago. *I hate to be the bearer of bad news, but I would advise the two of you not to try for more children. Another pregnancy will most likely end as your other two and I'm sure the loss hasn't been easy on either of you.* Although he hadn't said they would never have children, Donna knew in her heart it was true.

The vehicle rolled to a stop as Bobby parked the car in the driveway. His hand covered Donna's and she met his gaze.

"Are you okay, babe?"

She nodded even as she struggled against the urge to cry. "I'm fine."

"Are you sure?"

She nodded again.

Bobby slid toward her and kissed her lips. Then he

buried his face in her hair, wrapping his arms around her. "I love you, Donna."

"I love you too."

Bobby pulled back and caressed her cheek. His eyes met hers solemnly. "Even if we never have any children, I'll be content to just have you."

The tears won out this time, blurring her vision in silent victory.

Bobby pressed his mouth to hers, then dropped a kiss onto her forehead.

Donna leaned into him, allowing him to support her.

The crunch of tires on rocks brought her head up. A vehicle rolled toward them. Donna quickly swiped at her tears.

"Why don't you go on inside, Donna? I'll take care of it."

She nodded and exited the car. She didn't bother to glance back as she headed for the house. Hopefully, whoever it was wouldn't stay long.

Donna let herself in and found her feet moving of their own accord, leading her to their unoccupied bedroom–the nursery. She flicked on the lights and took in the crib in the corner, the little rocking horse Danny and Pamela had given them, the dresser full of baby clothes that had never been used.

Twice, she and Bobby had planned in this room. They'd discussed baby names while being surrounded by their future children's things. They'd decorated and painted the walls. They'd purchased countless toys and clothes. All for nothing.

Is this all my fault? Am I being punished, God? She couldn't help the thoughts that had replayed in her mind time and time again.

Bobby's voice, along with another, caught her attention. The voice seemed familiar, but Donna didn't bother to try to figure out who it might be.

"Donna?" Bobby called.

She stifled a groan and hoped Bobby wouldn't find her. She wasn't ready to entertain guests.

"Donna?" He was closer this time.

Footsteps neared the room as he said, "Maybe she's in the nursery." The door opened and Donna turned to her husband.

"There you are, Donna. You won't believe who's here!" Bobby fairly beamed as he stepped aside and she was able to see who stood behind him.

"Rick."

The word left her mouth in a whisper as she took in his familiar face and frame. Only, he wasn't as familiar as she remembered. The scar trailing from the corner of his right eye to his cheekbone was new. As was the hesitance holding him stiff.

"Hi, Donna." He smiled slightly.

"You're..."–she swallowed–"You're alive?"

"Yes."

"What are you doing here?" Her gaze shifted to Bobby. "What is he doing here?"

Bobby frowned. "Donna, what's wrong? I would think you'd be happy to see Rick."

Donna fought to rein in her emotions. She couldn't react now. Not in front of Bobby. "I'm just...surprised."

"I was too, but I didn't react like that." Bobby seemed puzzled at her behavior.

"It's alright, Bobby," Rick spoke up.

They stood there, crowded in the nursery, for what seemed like several awkward moments. Donna fought the waves of memories crashing through her mind. She needed to get away. She had to think. Finally, she could stand the silence no longer.

"Excuse me." She ducked her head and attempted to slip past Bobby and Rick.

"Wait, Donna, I didn't even tell you the best part."

She turned at her husband's words and met his gaze, avoiding eye contact with Rick.

"Rick's gonna stay here with us."

Her insides froze. "What?"

"He's staying with us. He didn't think he'd be welcomed in his folks' home. Danny and Pamela don't have much room in their small house, and it's just you and I here. It's the best place."

"No." She shook her head.

"Donna...listen, I already told Rick he could stay here."

"Where will he sleep?"

Donna chanced a glance at Rick who stood in regrettable silence.

Bobby gestured to the nursery. "In here, of course. It's our only guest room."

"It's not a guest room. It's for our babies. Not Rick."

"Donna, you're being rude." Bobby approached and gently gripped her forearms. His confused stare met her moist eyes. "For now, the room is empty, babe. Rick is going to use it."

She shook her head, fighting the tears threatening to fall.

"Donna, what—?"

Donna slipped from his grasp and rushed to their bedroom, shutting the door behind her.

Sixteen

"I don't want to cause trouble between you and Donna. Maybe this wasn't such a good idea. I shouldn't have come." Rick shook his head and mentally scolded himself for his lapse in judgment. "I can go, Bobby. Maybe it won't be so bad at my folks' place."

"No, you can stay here. I really could use a good friend right now."

Rick frowned. "Are you sure? Because I don't think your wife feels the same way."

"I'm sorry about that, Rick. I don't know what's come over Donna. I've never seen her act like that."

"Don't worry about it. I'm sure you're both under a lot of stress." Rick glanced at the empty crib in the corner and couldn't help but mourn for Bobby and Donna's loss. He'd only learned of it after he returned yesterday, thanks to Danny and Pamela filling him in on all the goings on. He'd crashed on their couch the night before but he felt like an interloper. He was beginning to get the same feeling here. Would he ever fit in again?

Bobby sighed and nodded. "I hope you never know what

it's like to lose your own child."

Noticing the turmoil in his friend's eyes, Rick clasped his shoulder. "How are you holding up, man?"

Bobby shrugged. "I'm alright. Getting by, at least. It's Donna that I'm worried about."

"I'm sure she'll recover. These things usually just take some time." Rick doubted the shock of Donna seeing him again had helped anything. Especially not how things had ended between them. He blew out a breath and did his best to *not* remember that night. "Maybe it would be best if I did just stay elsewhere. I'm sure Danny and Pamela wouldn't mind if I stayed there."

"No, it's fine, Rick. I mean it. You can stay. I want you here. Besides, Danny and Pamela are busy with their little ones so I'm sure you'll be able to get a lot more peace and quiet around here. Don't worry about Donna's reaction. I'm sure she'll eventually come to terms with the situation. Like you said, she just needs time." Bobby pulled out a folded bed from the closet. "I've got a bed for you right here. Unless you wanna sleep in the crib." He cocked a brow, a grin creeping up his face.

Rick frowned in concentration. "Well, I could try if you think that would be more comfortable. I might be a little too small for a crib though."

Bobby nodded. "Definitely too small."

A laugh escaped Rick, catching him by surprise. He hadn't laughed since he'd left the states. There was nothing funny about the battle in Vietnam. No, he hadn't laughed since the evening he and Donna... *Stop!*

Bobby turned back to the closet and handed him some fresh linens.

"Thanks, man. For everything." He smiled.

Bobby gripped his shoulders in a manly embrace. "I'm glad to have you back, friend."

Rick smiled. "You have no idea how good it feels to be home."

"I'm sure I don't." All mirth fled Bobby's face and Rick's insides froze.

Does Bobby know?

Bobby reached out and gripped Rick's forearm. "Thank you, man. For serving our country, fighting for the good. Not everybody appreciates your sacrifice, but I do. Thank you for doing what you did."

An overwhelming gratitude surfaced in the form of tears, which he struggled to conceal. Rick nodded, unable to form words.

Bobby turned and stepped out of the room. "You get a good night's rest now."

Bobby entered his and Donna's bedroom and Rick shut the nursery door. He rotated in a semi-circle and took in the small room. There was no disguising the bedroom's nursery status. Every inch of space screamed "baby," from the pale blue walls to the crib, rocking horse, and building blocks. He pulled open a dresser drawer and, sure enough, found folded baby clothes. The time and effort Bobby and Donna must have put into the room was staggering. There was no doubt any child they had would be well cared for.

Every square inch of the room seemed to condemn him

an outsider. It was no shock. Everyone considered him an outsider now. Even his own parents.

Rick sighed and shut off the light. He undressed in the darkness and lowered himself onto the folding bed.

In his camouflage pants and jacket, he was easily classified as military. It hadn't taken long for the dreaded stories he'd heard–of soldiers returning home to scorn and ridicule–to prove true. Many had been content to whisper and stare, to cover their children's eyes and turn up a nose at his presence. Others were not so easily avoided and preferred to make their distaste known. Vegetables seemed to be the object of choice when folks decided to make a target of him. Thankfully, not everyone had the aim of a Vietnamese soldier or he'd be in serious danger.

A sound jerked him upright in bed, had him reaching for his weapon. But there was no enemy ambushing him and his comrades. Only, he realized as the sound returned, a mouse hiding in the walls. He fell back on the mattress and shut his eyes to the darkness.

Thank You for bringing me home, God. Thank You for bringing me home.

....

Donna took the carafe of coffee, poured the hot liquid into two mugs, and set them on the table with fresh cream. The milk man had dropped off two bottles of milk the day before and there'd been extra cream on the top like she'd requested. That had always been a favorite of Bobby's, fresh cream with pure maple syrup, supplied by a woman at church who had relatives up in Vermont. Donna had to admit she enjoyed the combination as well. She had baked a cinnamon coffee cake–Bobby's favorite–early this morning and decided it would go perfectly with the coffee.

Donna released the breath she'd been holding and allowed herself to finally relax a bit. Thankfully, Bobby hadn't said much this morning. He seemed to be able to read her well most of the time. He must've known she needed time to sort things out, but he hadn't known the true reason for her behavior.

How was she supposed to handle Rick showing up out of the blue after all this time? She'd already come to terms with the reality that he might have been dead. Seeing him now was like seeing a ghost. The past had been buried, but somehow it had become unearthed and was now standing in front of her – forcing her to face things she'd tried so hard to forget.

She decided the best thing for her to do was to avoid Rick as much as possible. If she didn't have to look at him or talk to him, everything would be fine. She would simply pretend he wasn't there. After all, she'd become very good at pretending. And when she had to speak out of common courtesy, she would say only what was necessary.

....

After breakfast, Rick sat on a chair just inside the back door, tying the laces on his work boots. He purposely lingered in hopes of speaking with Donna. Since she'd been smiling this morning, he hoped it would be a good time to catch her alone. He glanced out the window of the back door and noticed Bobby fiddling under the hood of his car. Rick took one last swig of his coffee and neared the kitchen sink to place his empty mug on the counter. Donna had already begun washing the breakfast dishes.

"Donna, I wanted to say–"

"Don't you think Bobby's probably waiting for you outside?" she spat out. He noticed she was clenching her hands tightly in the dish water.

"I was hoping we could talk," he said gently. Rick wished she would just look at him and see the sincerity in his eyes. He genuinely desired to rectify past wrongs.

"No amount of talk can change anything, Rick. Now I think it's best that you go do whatever you and my husband have planned today. Bobby will wonder where you are," she answered curtly, then resumed her dish washing with vigor. "We wouldn't want him to think there was ever anything between us, would we?"

Rick sighed with a heavy heart and walked to the door in resignation. Yep, he'd read her correctly. She hadn't forgiven him for leaving the way he did. He couldn't say he blamed her, though. Regaining her friendship certainly wasn't going to be easy. At least he still had Bobby's friendship. Fortunately, all hadn't been lost.

....

"Oh, man. That was a great game! I hadn't gone bowling in ages, it seems." Bobby sipped his Coke and leaned back against the booth.

Rick laughed. "Yeah, but next time try not to drop the bowling ball on my foot."

"Hey, you know that was an accident. I'd never do something like that on purpose." Bobby shook his head. "I can't believe it just slipped out of my hand. I feel like I've had butterfingers all night."

"That's probably why I won!"

"I don't know how you got so many strikes." He glanced at Rick's empty glass. "Hey, you want more?"

"I guess I'll need some with my burger and fries." Rick smiled.

"Okay, I'll get us both a refill." Bobby rose from their booth and sauntered around the counter where the cash register stood.

"Hey, Bobby," his father called out from the back kitchen. "Rick's and your order is ready, if you'd like to take it to your table."

"Sure, Pops. Thanks for coming in today. I'm sorry it was short notice."

"Not a problem, son. You need a day off every now and then too. I'm just a little surprised you and Rick would come here to eat."

"Donna's not herself right now. I didn't want to burden her with having to make every meal for us." Bobby shrugged. "And Rick loves our food."

After refilling their drinks, he placed the hot plates and full glasses on a tray and moved back out to the dining area of the restaurant. He set a plate in front of his friend. "Your burger and fries, sir."

"Burger and fries? But I ordered meatloaf!" Rick protested, bringing his fist to the table.

"Did you, really?" Bobby's brow rose.

Rick laughed. "No. Just giving you a hard time is all."

Bobby mock-swiped his brow. "Shew! 'Cause I did not want to go in there and complain to the cook. He's a monster today."

"Really?"

"No." Bobby smiled. "You know how easygoing Pops is."

"I can't see him getting upset easily. He's always been quick with a smile."

"Yep, that's Pops." He sat the empty tray down on the vacant table next to him and took his seat across from Rick. "Man, it is so good to have you back home."

"Ah, it's good to be home."

"I can imagine. What was it like out there, man?"

"In Vietnam?" He shrugged. "It's war, you know? Nothing too glamorous about it. Guns, grenades, death– not really stuff you want to talk about."

"I've heard from other people that Vietnam is a beautiful place, with all the jungles and such."

"Yeah, the part that wasn't destroyed." Rick sighed. "Getting captured was the worst part. You never knew what they were going to do to you. Not too fun being at the mercy of the enemy."

"What *did* they do to you?"

Rick shook his head. "I'm sorry, man. I'd just rather not talk about it."

"I understand." Bobby nodded. "Hey, listen, if you ever want to talk..."

"I appreciate that. But right now, I'd rather just try to forget."

"Sure. Hey, how's your burger?"

"The best, as usual. You guys beat Mack's in the burger department any day."

"Thanks. I'll have to tell Pops that."

Seventeen

Donna chanced a glance out the window and saw Rick walking toward the house. Frustration built as he opened the door and walked in.

"Where's Bobby?" She frowned.

"He's in the garage working on the–"

Donna couldn't help her reaction to Rick. Seemingly of its own accord, her palm met Rick's left cheek with unrestrained ferocity.

"Ow!" Rick's hand immediately flew to his cheek.

Donna's hand now smarted as she noticed his face turning a wonderful satisfying shade of pink. It felt so good to finally relieve some of the frustration and bitterness she'd harbored in her heart over the last couple of years.

"I guess I deserved that." His shoulders slumped.

"You *guess*?" She should slap him again.

"Donna, can we talk? There are so many things I've wanted to say to you."

"It's a little late for that, don't you think?"

"I think maybe it will help both of us."

"No, it can never change what you did." She felt her

breathing go shallow as she thought back to that horrible time in her life–a time when Rick should have been there for her.

....

Bobby wasn't entirely sure, but he'd had a hunch that something must have happened between Rick and Donna that he was unaware of. Why on earth had Donna been so rude to Rick? It was almost as though she hated him. But what would she hate him for? Had he said something to offend her in some way? He'd never thought of Donna as the type of person that would be easily offended. That was the part that had him puzzled.

It seemed like Rick was trying to make amends, but so far he'd been unsuccessful. He guessed that was why he was taking longer than necessary to grab a drink.

Bobby set his wrench down and wiped his hands on his shop towel. There was a good chance Rick might need to be rescued right about now. And he could certainly use a drink himself as well. As he neared the house, he heard voices carrying through the window screens. Maybe he shouldn't interrupt. He stood just outside the kitchen window and listened to make sure he didn't butt in on something.

....

"I'm sorry." Rick frowned but Donna wasn't buying it.

She scoffed at his words.

"I don't know what to say, Donna."

Well, she did. She had a lot to say, actually. "How could

you do that? How could you just leave like that?"

"I had to, Donna. It's the United States military. If you've signed up, there's not much chance of getting out without serving your time."

"You left me alone after we..."

"I promise I meant everything I said that night. Donna, it killed me to have to go away and leave you so soon. I thought about you every day. If I hadn't gone into the military, I would have married you."

"Married me?" Her voice screeched and she shook her head as the moisture ran down her cheeks. How could he say this *now*? Why did he not state this fact in a letter? A telephone call? *Anything* at the time to stop her from what she'd done. Things could have been so different. She lifted her gaze to his, her eyes attempting to penetrate his soul. If she could only allay some of this guilt, transfer just a portion of this sorrow to Rick. Shouldn't *he* be bearing it as well? "Rick, we didn't just make love. We made a baby that night."

"A wha–a baby?"

She had a feeling that got his attention more than the slap on the face.

"But wha–how? I mean, where is it? Where is he? She?"

She shook her head as an avalanche of tears threatened.

"What do you mean 'no'?"

"I couldn't, Rick. I couldn't do it, not by myself. I couldn't have the baby on my own and bring shame to my father. If you would have been here..."

"What do you mean, you couldn't? What are you saying,

Donna? Did you go away and have the baby? Did you give it up for adoption?"

If only that were the case. Her hands began to shake and her bottom lip trembled so badly, she couldn't speak.

"Where is our baby?"

"She's dead." She hadn't been certain their baby was a girl, but that's what she'd always felt in her heart.

"Dead?"

She nodded matter-of-factly, trying to explain the horrifying event as though it didn't still shred her heart to pieces. "I went to a *doctor* and he removed it."

"He *removed* it? You mean, the baby was dead? You had a miscarriage?"

"No. He took the baby." She stared off into the distance. "She died."

"I'm sorry, Donna, but I'm not fully catching your vibe here."

A stern voice echoed from the door. "She had what's called an abortion. She had your baby murdered, Rick." *Bobby?*

No, God. Bobby can't know. Please. Donna looked at Bobby in dismay. She saw the disappointment in his eyes— the betrayal he felt. Her heart nearly stopped. How long had he been listening in on their conversation?

"You knew? You knew and you just let her kill my child?" Rick's mouth hung open and he turned from Bobby to Donna. "Donna, this isn't true, is it? It can't be. You didn't have our baby killed. *Please*, tell me you wouldn't do something like that."

Tears assaulted her once again. What could she say? It was true. It was all true.

Bobby frowned. "Nope, I had no clue. This is the first *I've* heard any of it. But the doctor explained abortion to me, and I'm quite certain that my wife had one." His hardened condemning gaze stabbed at her soul. "Aren't I correct, Donna? You and my best bud here had a little fling that resulted in the death of an innocent baby. Oh wait, make that *three* innocent babies. You killed *ours* too."

Donna burst into tears, or a wail was more accurate.

"Oh, I don't think crying is going to get you out of anything this time." Bobby's words mocked her. "I'm fed up with your crying."

If they'd only known how difficult it had been–if they could only put themselves in her shoes. She had to defend herself. She had to let them know that she wasn't the monster they thought she was. "I was all alone! What was I supposed to do?"

"Oh, I don't know. Keep your clothes on, maybe? Betrayed by my best friend and my best girl. Imagine that! I can't believe it. All that talk about wanting to wait for marriage and only wanting to please God. Baloney." Bobby sneered.

"I did want to. I'm sorry I'm not perfect."

Bobby turned to Rick, ignoring her comment. "How'd you do it, Rick? How'd you get Donna into bed? Because she sure wouldn't indulge me."

Rick spoke up. "That's enough, Bobby! I won't let you talk about Donna that way."

"You won't *let* me?" Bobby scoffed. "So, *now* he cares? But you didn't care about trying to steal my girl, did you?"

Donna cringed as Bobby's fist knocked Rick backwards. Rick returned Bobby's punch with a blow of his own to Bobby's jaw. Bobby grunted and charged at Rick full force until they both slammed up against the wall behind him. Bobby's fist crashed into Rick's stomach and he doubled over before delivering the same to his arch enemy.

"Stop it! Both of you!" Donna cried. "Just stop!"

"Why stop at three deaths, Donna? Let's make it an even four." Bobby's taunt earned him another blow from Rick. "What do you say, old friend? Fight to the death? Whichever of us wins gets my wife. How does that sound?"

"I don't want to fight you. And I don't want your wife."

Bobby howled. "Did you hear that, Donna? My good friend Rick here says he's done with you." Donna detested the sarcasm in Bobby's voice.

"That's not what I meant and you know it."

"Ah, so you're *not* done with her. I should have seen that one coming from a mile away. It's no wonder you moved in with us. Good move, buddy. That's been your plan the whole time, hasn't it? I wouldn't be surprised if you two have been sneaking around since you've been back."

"No, we haven't. Quit twisting my words!"

"The way you've twisted my life? It seems to me, you've already had your fun. I'm entitled to a little, aren't I?"

Donna knew Bobby's words stemmed from the hurt and betrayal he was feeling inside. She couldn't blame him. In fact, she deserved much worse. Her heart now seemed as though it were plunging into an abyss of hopelessness. What had she done? Bobby's words were harsh, but they were the truth. She had, in fact, killed three innocent human beings due to her one selfish act. Instead of admitting her sin, she'd attempted to cover it up. How many times had she been warned against the pitfalls of sin?

Be sure your sin will find you out. Scriptures began running through her head. *He that covereth his sins shall not proper: but whoso confesseth and forsaketh them shall have mercy.* Why hadn't she just humbled herself, gone to her father, and confessed? Why had she let fear take hold of her to the point she was willing to end the life of an innocent human being? The Bible was so right.

If only she could go back and do things differently. If only she would have chosen the good and right thing. But it was too late for that. None of the things of the past could be changed now. All she had was the present and the future. She could either admit her wrongdoing and bear the shame or she could continue to live a lie.

I call heaven and earth to record this day against you, that I have set before you life and death, blessing and cursing: therefore choose life, that both thou and thy seed may live. Oh, if only she'd chosen life–chosen the blessing. But she hadn't. She'd chosen death. She'd *chosen* the curse.

God, forgive me!

Eighteen

Bobby couldn't help the cold stare he gave Donna.

How could she have done that? How could she just give herself away to his best friend? And then...their children. The ones who were now buried in the ground, their precious babies who'd never taken their first breath. An image of Robert Jr's lifeless body, as he'd held him in his arms, flashed through his mind.

A mixture of rage and heartache rose within him, so strong he shook beneath the weight of it. How could the two people he loved most betray him so thoroughly? Suddenly, he could no longer stand to look at either of them. At Rick–the Judas. Or at Donna–the Jezebel. "Get out, get out, get out!"

Donna's tear-filled eyes flew wide. "What?"

It figured she'd play dumb. How had he ever thought her innocence was genuine? She certainly had pulled the wool over his eyes. "I said, get out! Out of my house and off my property! I never want to see either of you ever again!" He didn't care if the entire neighborhood overheard his irate outburst. It was only a minute fraction of the turmoil that festered inside.

"Bobby, *please*." Donna's imploring tone grated and his temper boiled.

"Stop it, Donna! Just stop it! Didn't you hear me? I'm setting you free. Now you can go live with my back-stabbing best friend like you've always wanted."

"Bobby..." This came from Rick, who had no right to even open his mouth. Bobby shoved another fist into his *friend's* face. The sudden release of anger brought such satisfaction it was no wonder people made a living out of prizefighting. Perhaps he'd join the ranks once Rick and Donna cleared out.

A hand touched his arm and he whirled, fist raised. The fear in Donna's countenance made him pause. He could never hit Donna. No matter how she betrayed him, no matter how little she obviously cared for him, he couldn't do it.

He loved her.

Even in the face of her treachery, he loved her. She was practically a harlot, certainly a murderer, and most likely an adulteress too, and yet he couldn't make himself hate her. All he saw was the girl he once knew. The one who laughed at his jokes, whose face lit with joy when he proposed, who protested when their kisses got out of hand. Why couldn't she still be that sweet, innocent girl? The girl he *thought* he'd married.

He lowered his fist and met Donna's gaze.

Fear, guilt, shame, despair, anguish, helplessness. It was all there in her eyes. The beautiful blue eyes that crinkled when she laughed, draped shut when she was kissed.

A sudden, ridiculous desire took hold of him and he captured Donna's face between his hands before meeting her lips one last time. She tasted like dreams and paradise, like she always did. It was unfair, how her cheeks were just as soft as always beneath his palms, that her lips were just as sweet, even after they had been shared.

Shared. Disgust forced him away and the poison of her mouth on his now scalded him. He'd wanted to love her one last time and he had, but somewhere along the way, the beauty became tainted–the pure, soiled. Something akin to bile welled in his throat and Bobby heaved into the kitchen trash. Donna's love, which he had once thought sacred and precious, was now so ugly and cheap, it sickened him.

The tumult in his stomach began to subside while the turmoil in his mind and heart raged on. "Go."

The raw emotion in his voice surprised Bobby and he suspected Donna and Rick too, because neither of them said a word while their retreating footsteps announced what they were doing–going to their rooms to pack.

Bobby stared into the window above the sink, his eyes not seeing, his ears not hearing. Instead, he remembered.

He pressed his mouth to hers and kissed her so thoroughly by the time he pulled back for a breath, he was nearly dizzy with exhilaration. "Oh Donna, how I love you."

Their wedding night.

He remembered the look in Donna's eyes, the hesitance that was nearly fearful. At least, that's how he'd interpreted it.

"What's wrong, baby?"

"Bobby, I..."

He nuzzled her neck, touched his lips to her collarbone. "What is it?"

She bit her slightly swollen bottom lip. "I'm kind of scared."

"Don't be, precious. There's nothing scary about love. Nothing at all." He kissed her again, then rested his forehead on hers for a moment. "How can I be so blessed to have someone as beautiful and wonderful as you for my wife?"

He longed for the naïveté of that moment, the naïveté he possessed a mere hour ago. Before he'd learned that his wife, his world, had...

Acid rose within him, but this time, he wrestled it back down. The curse that followed was even harder to keep inside.

What is taking them so long?

An eternity seemed to pass him by as he stood there, arms braced on the countertop, back to the kitchen and the rest of the house.

Quiet footsteps traveled through the hallway. Donna, walking to Rick's bedroom. She was going to him, was now in the same room as him. *Are they kissing at this moment? Do they not even have the decency to wait until they have some privacy?*

Bobby gripped the counter so tightly he feared it would crack.

Finally, they left his room, walked through the hallway, through the living room... The footsteps paused when they reached the kitchen.

Bobby remained silent, the weight of their stares stiffening his body.

"Bobby, *please*..." It was Donna, her words trembling.

Then Rick, resignation coating his voice. "Come on, Donna. Let's not make this any harder than it is. Let's just go."

The door opened and then shut, plunging the house in silence. Unable to stop himself, Bobby watched as they headed for Rick's car. They set their suitcases in the back, then rounded the vehicle. Rick held the passenger door open for Donna and Bobby turned away from the sight in disgust.

Chivalry at its finest. Rick could apply for a position with the Knights of the Round Table with manners like that. Yet somehow Bobby doubted sleeping with your best friend's fiancé was in their code of ethics. Though he seemed to recall something about King Arthur's most trusted knight taking off with his wife. Suddenly, it seemed he and the legendary king had a lot in common.

The rumbling of an engine froze him in place. His eyelids shut as he listened to the vehicle containing his joy, his hopes and dreams, his past life, back out of the driveway and leave. The silence that followed was like an emptiness that continued to grow, widening and turning more and more of his world into nothingness.

He opened his eyes and looked around, walking into the living room. There was nothing. Simply furniture and walls. How had this become his world?

The sudden stinging of tears surprised him. He could count on one hand the number of times he'd cried in his life. Not many, that was certain. The day Donna broke up with him, on their wedding day, when their first baby was born dead, when their second child died, and now. It figured that each instance was somehow undeniably linked to Donna.

His wife, the traitor.

A trembling took over his limbs and Bobby sank onto the carpet. A deep grief unlike anything he had ever known seeped into his veins, racing to his heart and ripping it into tiny shreds. The torment stretched on and on, making seconds feel like an eternity. Immeasurable pain caused his heart to spasm and he choked on the sobs that rose from somewhere deep within him.

Bobby wondered if this was what it was like to die of a broken heart. The numberless tears, blurred vision, shaking body. And the internal symptoms: throbbing anguish, ugly helplessness, and a pit of sorrow so deep one could fall in and never be able to climb out. He couldn't imagine any worse death.

Somewhere, somehow, his vision focused on the coffee table. On it rested a thick, black book. His Bible.

Like a man in the desert rushing to an oasis, Bobby reached for his Bible. He opened it with shaky fingers. He looked down and read a verse that he had once underlined. *My grace is sufficient for thee; for my strength is made perfect in weakness.*

As though God Himself had just spoken those words aloud, an inexplicable peace washed over Bobby and he held out his hands in offering. "All I have is weakness, God. If you can make something perfect out of it, please...please do. Heal me, Jesus. Hold me. All I have is weakness."

New tears sprung to Bobby's eyes, but these were rooted in joy. The joy of knowing that his Saviour was always there for him, no matter what he went through. With Jesus in his heart, he was never and would never be alone.

Nineteen

A bass drum pounded in Donna's chest and it seemed as though all the air in the car suddenly disappeared. *Please don't leave me, Bobby.* She couldn't stop the barrage of tears as she buried her face in her hands. This was something that couldn't be fixed. Not something she could wish away or a nightmare that she'd eventually awaken from. This was real.

A moment later, she felt strong arms encircle her as she wept. Rick must've pulled the vehicle off the side of the road. He scooted next to her and quietly smoothed her hair as she sobbed in his arms. It seemed like an hour had passed, by the time the tears stopped flowing.

"I don't know what I'm going to do now. How will I tell my father that Bobby left me? He doesn't know about any of this. No one does. Just you, me, and now Bobby. I never wanted him to find out. I wanted to keep it buried until I died."

"I'm sorry, Donna. I feel like I'm to blame for all of this."

"No, you're not. You didn't force me, Rick. And you had no idea that I was pregnant."

"But still. I was careless. If I would have thought about the fact that I was going into the military, I would have stopped us."

She shook her head. "Do you really think you–we–would have stopped?"

"If I'd known that we'd lose a child because of it–" The pain in Rick's eyes didn't help to assuage Donna's guilt one bit. She'd disappointed him. Rick actually wanted his baby–their baby.

"But you didn't. There's no way you could have known. It *is* all my fault. I sacrificed our baby on the altar of pride, of fear, of uncertainty, of selfishness. I didn't care about an innocent life suffering because of my decision or how *you* would feel about it. I only thought about my own suffering. It's indefensible, really. I've been trying to excuse it away in my mind all these years and it just refuses to go away. I messed up."

"We both did. You wouldn't even have been in that condition if it weren't for me. I wish I could have at least been here for you. Man, I've failed everybody. I failed Bobby. I failed my folks. I failed you. I failed our baby. I'm a *total* failure." He sighed. "Donna, I had every intention to marry you upon my return. But I hadn't expected to be gone so long, and the war... well, I'd rather not talk about that." He shook his head and Donna noted the turmoil in his eyes. "I think somewhere deep in my heart I knew you would go back to Bobby."

"I had no idea you felt that way. If I had, I probably would have waited for you. But you left. And I thought you didn't care. I thought you just wanted to have some fun before you shipped off to wherever."

"No, Donna. That night was as much of a surprise to me as it was to you. All I'd hoped for was a game of Parcheesi and to see you smile again after your breakup with Bobby. I didn't even expect you to kiss me. I had no idea that we would..." He reached for her hand and gently squeezed it. "I wasn't looking for one last hurrah. In my heart, I've always loved you deeply. I've always wanted to be with you. To me, the time we spent together far exceeded all my dreams. But I never intended it to be a one-time thing. I hoped it would be the first night of many for years to come. Till death do us part, you know?"

"I...I don't know what to say."

"Donna, this might not be the time or the place but I need to say it. If you and Bobby do end your marriage, I would still be honored to have you for my wife."

She searched his eyes. "Do you mean that?"

"With all my heart."

"I'm unworthy of your kindness."

"No. If anyone is unworthy, it's me."

....

Pamela's head spun around as an ambulance whizzed by. "Oh, no. I wonder what happened. Do you think it's someone we know?"

"Could be. In small towns, you can usually count on it." Danny nodded and waited patiently for the long line of cars ahead of them. He tapped the steering wheel. "It looks like it might have been an accident."

"I hate accidents."

Danny chuckled. "I don't know anyone who adores them."

She playfully slapped his arm. "You know what I mean."

He smiled. "I don't know about you, but I am really looking forward to this date tonight."

"Me, too. If we ever make it there."

The traffic was now at a complete standstill.

"We may have to call your father and tell him we're going to pick the kiddos up a little late." Danny reached over and caressed her leg. "Maybe we can have him keep them overnight."

Pamela smiled and indulged him with an enticing kiss.

The car behind them honked and Pamela jumped back.

Danny laughed. "I guess we should probably save that for later, huh?"

Pamela loved the pink that stained his cheeks.

Traffic now began to move as the roadway cleared. A tow-truck passed them hauling a station wagon. A moment later, another tow-truck passed.

"Oh, my goodness! That looked just like your brother's car!"

Danny frowned. "You're right. It did."

As soon as they reached the emergency vehicles, Danny pulled off the side of the road. He jumped out and approached the officer. "Who was in the red vehicle? It looked like my brother's car."

The officer scratched his head and set down the suitcase he was holding. "A young man, looked to be around your age and a young woman about the same."

"That looks like Donna's suitcase, Danny!" Pamela stood beside him.

"May we look inside?" Danny asked the officer.

"I guess that would be okay." The officer shrugged. "I'll have to open it for you, though. Don't touch anything."

The moment he opened it, Pamela knew. "Oh, no! Those are Donna's things."

Danny looked at her and frowned. "You're sure?"

"Positive." Pamela nodded.

"Let's get to the hospital."

....

Pamela and Danny hastily walked into the hospital in search of Rick and Donna. It was difficult to believe she'd just been there just a couple of months ago to see Donna and now she was back again. When Pamela noticed nobody in attendance at the information desk, she was ready to pull her hair out. She impatiently rang the brass bell on top of the counter. Danny's comforting hand rubbed her back although she knew he was still in shock from learning of the accident. She rang the bell again and when nobody answered they set out to find a nurses' station.

As their feet pounded the corridor, Pamela's mind whirled. Where were Rick and Donna going? Where was Bobby? Why did Donna have her suitcase with her? Then another thought occurred to her. Were Rick and Donna running off together? To Pamela, the thought seemed preposterous. She had warned Donna about Rick living with them, but she never thought that they would do something like that. Rick and Donna were both levelheaded and responsible. Pamela couldn't imagine the two of them doing anything of the sort, it was simply uncharacteristic.

Pamela was shaken from her thoughts when they arrived at the nurses' station. A plump woman with graying hair and hot pink spectacles looked up as they approached. "My sister, Donna Dillon, and his brother, Rick Landers, they were in an accident not too long ago," Pamela uttered.

"You'll need to exit this building and enter the emergency wing on the north side of Building A. They're both in ICU right now, but I don't have any details. Chances are, you won't be able to see them for a while if they were recently admitted," the nurse advised.

"Thank you." Pamela turned to go.

"Uh, if you want I can call and try to get a little more information before you walk all the way over there. I'd hate to have you go all that way just to find out that you can't see them," the friendly nurse said.

"Thank you, we would appreciate that," Danny spoke.

The woman suggested they take a seat while she picked up the telephone and dialed a number. A moment later she called them back over to the window. "Donna is in surgery now and probably won't be out till late tonight. She'll be under anesthesia so you most likely won't be able to get in to see her until tomorrow."

"And Rick?" Danny's voice worried.

"You won't be able to see him, either, I'm afraid."

"But he's alive?" Poor Danny. If Pamela didn't know better, she'd think he was more concerned than she was.

"Yes, honey. He's alive."

Danny exhaled.

Pamela frowned. She stepped up to the window to speak with the nurse once again. "What is Donna having surgery for? Is my sister going to be okay?"

"I'm not certain, dear. I'm sorry I don't have more information for you. You may call back in the morning to check whether they will be allowing visitors or not."

"Thank you. We will return tomorrow," Danny said, gently grasping Pamela's elbow. "Let's go, Pamela. We must tell Mom and Dad about Rick and Donna. And Bobby and your father will want to know about them, I'm sure."

Pamela didn't put up a fight. Besides, she was anxious to talk to Bobby about Donna and set her mind at ease as to why Rick and her sister were riding alone in Rick's car.

....

After breaking the news about the accident to Danny's folks, Pamela's head was still filled with unanswered questions. While Rick's parents knew Donna was involved in the accident, nobody dared bring up the fact that she and Rick had been traveling together alone. Danny was at a loss as well, and Pamela determined not to worry him further with her speculations. Only three people held the answers to her questions: Donna and Rick who were incapacitated at the moment and in no condition to be interrogated, and Bobby.

When Pamela and Danny arrived at the Dillon residence, they'd first scanned the property expecting Bobby to be working on his car or some other task. After determining he wasn't in the garage or the backyard, they decided to try the house. They knocked on the door twice, but Bobby did not open it.

Pamela frowned at her husband. "Do you suppose something is wrong?"

"He should be here. His car is in the garage," Danny said.

"Let's just go in," Pamela said, pushing the door open before Danny had a chance to object.

The house seemed quiet–too quiet. Something wasn't right. Pamela rushed to Donna and Bobby's bedroom and gasped when she saw Donna's things strewn everywhere. The chaotic room caused Pamela's heart to plunge. Her sister never would have left the house in this condition. Had there been a burglar in the house? Or had something terrible happened between Bobby and Donna?

"This doesn't look too good, Pamela," Danny commented behind her.

"Danny, what do you think happened? You don't suppose Donna and Bobby had a fight?" She voiced her thoughts.

The sound of a music box drew their attention down the hallway. They quickly but cautiously walked to where they'd heard the sound. Danny gingerly opened the door to the spare bedroom where Bobby sat on the floor near the bed with his head in his hands.

Pamela frowned as she thought of the babies that would never occupy this nursery. Poor Donna and Bobby, they had been through so much already. It pained her heart to think that they might be going through even more turmoil.

"Bobby, are you all right?" Danny asked.

Bobby looked up with bleary red-rimmed eyes, his face contorted with pain. "They're gone." His bottom lip trembled as he said the words.

Never in her life had Pamela seen Bobby in such a state. He'd always been calm and confident, even when Donna had her troubles. "What happened?"

"Your sister and his brother left together. The last I saw of them they were talking about marriage." Bobby's disgusted tone evidenced his bitterness. "I'm through with both of them." That explained the disaster in the bedroom.

Donna and Rick talking of marriage? Surely Bobby must be mistaken. Pamela couldn't imagine it. *Oh no. Lord, please tell me they weren't committing adultery this whole time.*

"Bobby, Donna and Rick were in an accident. They're both in the intensive care at the hospital," Danny said.

Bobby eyed them both wearily. Indifferent, he shrugged. "So be it."

Enraged, Pamela raised her voice, "Don't you even care that your best friend and your wife were in an accident? They could die, Bobby."

"I don't have a wife or a best friend anymore. They are already dead to me."

Danny and Pamela looked at each other helplessly. It was clear that they weren't going to be able to get through to Bobby, especially in his current state. Maybe Danny could talk to Bobby after he'd calmed down some and they knew all the facts. And as soon as Donna was able, Pamela was going to have a talk with her older sister to find out what exactly happened. She refused to believe that Donna would have an immoral relationship with another man–any man– while she was married to Bobby. Surely there must be some logical explanation.

Twenty

Pamela had tossed and turned all night. She might as well have stayed at the hospital since she wasn't going to get any sleep anyway. Of course she hadn't known that beforehand, but she should have figured. After visiting Bobby last night, she and Danny had informed her father about the accident. Daddy was presently at the hospital waiting for Donna to awaken.

She hadn't told Daddy about Bobby's state of mind or what he'd said about Donna and Rick. Pamela knew she should first talk to Donna and find out what actually happened between her, Rick, and Bobby. If what Bobby said was indeed true, she couldn't blame him for being upset.

As they now walked the corridor of the hospital, Pamela worried about what might be awaiting them. She knew hospitals were a necessary part of life, but that didn't make her hate them any less. It seemed that bad things always tended to happen there–like when they'd found out Momma had died.

After learning that Rick was in a coma, Danny agreed he would go and talk with Bobby sometime today. As soon as they discovered the truth from Donna, he'd set out to console Bobby. They'd been too exhausted, both physically and emotionally, to deal with him last night.

As Pamela now entered Donna's hospital room, she shared a sympathetic look with Daddy, who'd been sitting at Donna's bedside. He quietly motioned her out into the hallway.

"I'm worried about her, Pamela. She's been awake for two hours now and hasn't said more than two words to me," he said anxiously.

"What has she heard about the accident? Does she know about Rick?" Pamela asked cautiously, not wanting to give too much away.

"She knows she was in a car accident, but I don't think she knows that Rick's in a coma. I'm not sure if she fully understands what happened. The doctors have her on pain medication, so that might be clouding her thinking."

"Perhaps. Daddy, would you mind if I have some time alone with Donna?" Pamela asked.

"No. I've been dying to go downstairs to the cafeteria, but I didn't want to leave Donna's side. The doctors said that she'd be able to go home at the end of the week. Other than a slight concussion, a few stitches, and a fractured wrist, I'd say Donna escaped pretty well," Daddy said. "They thought she might need surgery, but they decided against it. Thank God."

"God must have been looking out for her," Pamela agreed.

Pamela watched Daddy head down the hallway. She took

a deep breath, said a quick prayer, and then entered Donna's room. Donna didn't bother to turn her head when she came in, but instead stared at the wall in front of her. She appeared sallow and disheartened. Pamela debated whether to share Rick's condition with her or not.

"Donna, how are you doing?" Pamela reached out and touched her sister's arm.

Donna glanced at Pamela, then a lone tear trickled down her cheek.

Pamela walked over to Donna and gave her an awkward hug, trying not to bump her injured wrist. "Shh...it'll be all right, Donna," she said, attempting to comfort her sister.

"Rick? Where...where is he, Pamela?"

Like it or not, she was going to have to be honest with Donna. She gave her sister a sympathetic look and her own eyes filled with tears. "Rick is in a coma, Donna. They say he might not make it."

"No! He can't die." Donna shook her head. "He can't do that to me, Pamela. Haven't I paid enough for my sin already? Will God take Rick too? He's all I have left," Donna cried. "I wish He'd taken me. Why won't He let me die too?"

"What do you mean? What sin are you paying for? I don't understand, Donna. Please, help me understand." Pamela frowned.

"I killed Rick's baby, Pamela," Donna cried miserably.

Pamela figured the medication Donna was taking must be confusing her thoughts. "What do you mean? Rick didn't have any children."

Donna nodded. "Nobody knew about it. When Rick left for the military, I was expecting his baby. That's why I was so sick back then. I was scared, Pamela. I thought Rick didn't love me and I didn't know if he'd even return. I didn't know what to do, so I talked to a nurse and..." Her voice trailed off, giving way to sobs.

"You were expecting a baby at eighteen?" Pamela couldn't believe the words she was hearing. How could Donna, perfect Donna, have gotten pregnant? And with *Rick's* baby nonetheless. Rick and Donna were two of the most saintly people she knew. Wow, a bomb dropping from the sky couldn't have shocked her more. "Rick didn't know?"

Donna found her voice. "The baby was conceived the day before he shipped off. We had no way of knowing at the time. He only found out about it yesterday."

"And what about Bobby?"

"He found out too." Donna brushed away another tear. "The doctor said that's the reason I keep losing my babies. I was damaged during the procedure. Pamela, I can't ever have a baby now. My life is ruined. Bobby doesn't love me anymore. And now if Rick doesn't make it..." Her breathing became shallow. "I know as soon as everyone else finds out, they will despise me too. Why do I have to live, Pammy? I don't understand. Why won't God kill me? I just want to go be with Momma. I just want to die."

Tears streamed down Pamela's cheeks as she pulled her sister close and held her tight. She couldn't fathom the emotional pain and guilt Donna must be experiencing. No wonder her sister had been so melancholy all the time. To have carried this secret around all those years must've been excruciating. And then to blame herself for everything bad that had happened since then. Pamela realized that her sister needed more help than what she could offer, but she attempted to console her anyway.

"No, Donna. Please don't ever say that. No one wants you to die. We love you. You were young and desperate and you made a mistake." She stroked her sister's hair. "We all mess up, Donna. All these things that have happened since then are not your fault. You couldn't have known it would affect your life this way. And regardless of how you may feel, God still loves you tremendously."

"I can't do it anymore, Pammy. I can't go on." Donna's hopelessness gripped Pamela's heart.

"You can, Donna. You can. I'll help you, okay? Your life *will* get better."

Pamela realized that she was not going to be able to penetrate the darkness that surrounded Donna's soul. She desperately needed professional spiritual help from someone who could relate to her circumstances. But Pamela had never personally known of anyone that had gone through an abortion. It wasn't exactly something that people shouted from the rooftops, especially since she was quite certain that something like that was illegal. No, Pamela suspected that there were probably many more women in Donna's shoes than she realized. How many of the people that she encountered on a daily basis carried around the silent pain of a secret abortion?

....

Danny had been thankful to finally hear the truth of the matter. When Rick awakened from his coma, he'd explained everything. Rick had also prompted him to visit Bobby and attempt to smooth things over. Danny knew that his brother still harbored a deep love for Donna, but he also realized that Donna didn't belong to him no matter how much he wished it were so.

As Danny now sat in Bobby and Donna's living room, he was thankful to get a chance to converse openly with Bobby. His friend had been in such a traumatic state before, he didn't believe he would have been able to think coherently. But now that Bobby had had some time to reflect, his attitude had gentled.

"Bobby, you can wish and pray all you want, but the reality is there is not one thing you can do to change the past. We all make mistakes. We all do stupid things at one time or another." Danny sighed. "You need to let this go. If not for Donna's sake, then for your own."

"I don't know, Danny. How in the world can I forgive something like that? I mean, my wife and my best friend? I feel like my heart has been ripped out and trampled on. It is because of them that I will never have the opportunity to raise children, to hear someone call me 'Dad.'" Bobby obviously attempted to squelch the emotion in his voice.

"I can imagine it must be hard." Danny frowned. "Did Donna ever explain the circumstances of her and my brother coming together?"

"No. And I never asked." He spat the words out.

"Bobby, it was after you proposed to Donna and she had just found out that *you'd* been cheating on *her*. She felt betrayed. And she thought your relationship was over. Donna had no idea that Rick would be leaving for Vietnam, so she thought they would go steady and get married. She'd already given your ring back, so in a way, she didn't *really* cheat on you."

"I never knew that."

"As far as Rick goes, Donna was fair game. Don't get me wrong, I'm *not* saying that what they did was right by any means. But Rick was there for her when she needed someone. And I know that my brother had had a crush on Donna forever. Since before you ever moved to town."

"Really? He never said anything. Why hadn't he asked her out before?"

"Well, Rick wasn't as outgoing as you were—especially when it came to girls. I think he sort-of gave up on Donna when you came along and asked her out."

Bobby frowned.

"Anyway, when Donna told Rick she'd broken up with you, I think he saw it as an opportunity to get to know her better. He said he never intended what happened between them, but it *did* happen."

Bobby squeezed his eyes shut. "It is *so* hard to forgive."

"Bobby, let me tell you something I've learned that I think might help you too. *You* hold the key to your own happiness. As a matter of fact, each of us does. Only you can choose to forget the hurts of the past and move on. Only you can choose forgiveness and healing. But the choice *is* yours.

It lies in your hands. You can choose to take the key and unlock the prison door, or you can pretend the key doesn't exist and let it sit untouched where it rusts away, as will your heart."

"Even if I did choose to forgive, I don't think Donna would want me back. Now that she has a chance with Rick ..."

"Last I heard, you and Donna were still married. Not that I don't want my brother to be happy, but she belongs to you. She's *your* wife. I couldn't imagine letting Pamela go off with another man. I don't care who he is." He shook off the disgusting thought. "It's the trials in our lives that make the relationships with the ones we love grow stronger. The truth is, Donna's a mess. She needs you to be strong now more than ever. She needs you to fight for your marriage because she doesn't have the strength to right now. I'm confident that if you can get through this, Bobby, you and Donna will be able to get through anything."

....

Bobby had trouble processing Danny's words.

Was there really hope that he and Donna could possibly have a decent marriage after all? Bobby couldn't help the tears in his eyes. "I'm willing to try to salvage this marriage if Donna is."

Danny's hand squeezed his shoulder. "That's great to hear. I'm proud of you, Bobby."

"No, I've been a jerk."

"Maybe so, but you can change. Speaking of change, I plan to have another chat with my brother."

Twenty-One

Danny walked into Rick's hospital room, dreading the task ahead of him. His brother had loved Donna for so long, he couldn't imagine this being an easy thing. For any of them.

"Hey, brother. How are you feeling?"

Rick shrugged and Danny sensed the action to be painful. "Like I got hit by a train."

"I think it was a station wagon, actually."

"Yeah. That and Bobby's fist." He grimaced.

He pivoted from one foot to the other. "We need to talk about something."

"I know. What Donna and I did before I shipped off to Nam was—"

"No, that's not what I'm referring to."

"Then, what?" His brow shot up.

"Rick, you've got to let Donna go."

Rick shook his head. "No. I am *not* giving her up. Not now."

"Look at me, Rick." Danny commanded and waited until he had his brother's full attention. "Donna doesn't belong to you. She's married to Bobby."

"Bobby." Rick nodded, his lips pressed firmly together and his fists balled at his sides. "You should have heard how Bobby spoke to her, Danny! He doesn't love her–not like I do. I'd never speak to any woman that way. Especially not Donna. She loves me too."

"Rick, listen. Donna and Bobby are still married, whether you like it or not."

"But they can get a divorce."

"Is that *really* what you want? You think about that for a few minutes, brother."

"It's what has to happen."

"No. Bobby is willing to work things out with Donna."

Rick frowned. "He is?"

"Yes. And I encouraged him to."

"Why?" His brother stared at him and he shook his head. Clearly he felt betrayed.

"Because it was the *right* thing to do. It's what God would've wanted me to do."

Tears sprang to Rick's eyes and he shook his head. "I don't want to let her go again. I love her *so* much."

"If you *truly* love her, you'll encourage her to go back to Bobby. Her husband." Danny sympathized with his brother. He couldn't imagine being on any side of this equation. Either way it worked, someone would end up losing. Unfortunately, this time it would be his brother.

....

It had been a feat in itself just to walk to Donna's hospital room, but Rick had to speak with her. A battle raged inside his soul as he stood gazing upon a resting Donna. Oh, how he loved her!

She moved slightly and Rick reached over and grasped her hand. "How are you holding up?"

Donna shrugged in silence.

Rick frowned. Donna looked so forlorn. He hated seeing her in this fog of depression. Where was the old Donna? The one who always had a smile or a word of encouragement? "I think you should go back to Bobby."

She shook her head. "No. *Please*, I want to be with you, Rick."

Oh, how he'd longed to hear those words. If he wasn't a Christian man, he might have just said, let's go. But he couldn't. Danny had been right. He knew that Donna didn't belong to him. She was Bobby's wife. The right thing to do was to encourage her to go back to him.

"Please, Rick. Bobby doesn't love me anymore. He can't even stand to see me." She brushed away a tear. "I thought you said you wanted to marry me."

"You have no idea how many times I've dreamed of marrying you. And I did mean it when I said that if things didn't work out between you and Bobby, I would love to have you as my wife." He pivoted from one foot to the other. "But, Donna, your marriage *isn't* over. You have to at least give it another try. If I know Bobby, he still loves you. He spoke those words to you out of anger and fear. He was afraid he would lose you."

"You're right."

Rick spun around at the sound of Bobby's voice. "Uh, Bobby, I..."

Bobby forced a smile. "May I have a word with my wife?"

"Yes, of course." Rick squeezed Donna's hand and nodded to her in reassurance. "It'll work out, you'll see. Goodbye, Donna."

He closed the hospital door with more than a tinge of regret. Who would have thought that he and Bobby would one day be enemies—or that he would willingly give up the woman of his dreams when he could have had her for his own? Certainly not him. But it had been the right thing to do. He did it out of love, and because of that, it lifted the aching in his heart just a little. *Please help me through this, Lord.*

....

Donna couldn't make herself meet Bobby's gaze. After all that he'd said before, she was certain he had nothing but more words of condemnation for her and she didn't think she could bear any more pain. Especially since she deserved every bit of it.

"Donna, I'm so sorry."

The sincerity in his tone aroused her curiosity and she chanced a peek at her husband. Tears glistened in his eyes. He stepped closer to her hospital bed.

"I've been such a fool. I have no right to condemn you when I've messed up so badly. I should have been there for you, all those years ago *and* a couple days ago. Instead, all I thought about was how *I* felt. I was so selfish and prideful."

Tears pooled into her eyes as well.

"Please forgive me, Donna. I've failed you in so many ways. I'm so sorry."

Donna covered his hand with hers. "I should be the one asking for your forgiveness, Bobby. I've caused all this chaos. I've destroyed our chances of having children. I've hurt you. I don't deserve your forgiveness, Bobby."

Bobby shook his head. "None of us deserve forgiveness. That's why it's so precious. I've forgiven you. Do you think you can find it in your heart to forgive me?"

Donna nodded. "Yes, of course."

Bobby leaned toward her and Donna wrapped her arms around him. She breathed in his familiar strength and comfort–a comfort she'd believed was gone forever–and burst into tears. "I don't want to let you go."

Bobby lifted her out of the hospital bed, conscious of her IV, and sat down on the bed, holding her close. He stroked her hair. "You don't have to, Donna. I want to stay married. I don't want a divorce. I want to start over, without any secrets. Do you want that too?"

She nodded, a sense of peace flooding her soul.

"We can never get back what we had. We won't ever be the same. But we can still have a good life together."

"I want that," Donna whispered. "More than anything else in the world."

Twenty-Two

Bobby dipped his toe in the sand, penned Donna's name, and then erased it. He contemplated his impending meeting with Rick, which was scheduled for just a few minutes from then. If only they could get back to the fun, easy friendship they used to have before things got complicated. It was true that he'd forgiven Rick, but he didn't know if he could ever trust him again. And trust had to be the foundation of any relationship.

He was slowly building that now with Donna, although he admitted it wasn't easy by any stretch of the word. No, each time she left the house alone, he'd worried that she might be stealing away to go meet Rick. When he left for work in the morning, he was anxious about what could transpire if Rick happened to stop by the house. Not that they would rush to the bedroom. No, but he knew that the heart could be stirred with the slightest action. A word. A look. A touch.

Since their relationship was on shaky ground, he didn't want to do anything that would make Donna want to run back into Rick's arms. Because, if Bobby admitted it to himself, Rick was a better man than he was. He was kinder, gentler, everything that Bobby wasn't. He sometimes wondered what Donna actually saw in him.

God, please help Donna and me. Strengthen our feeble marriage. Help me to make amends with Rick, and please restore our relationship as only You can.

"Hey, Bobby."

He looked up and spied Rick walking up the beach toward him, a surfboard under his arm. He looked down at his watch and shook his head. "Late as usual, I see."

Rick met his stare, probably to see whether he was joking or not.

Bobby smiled and offered his hand in greeting. "I'm kidding. You're actually two minutes early."

"Oh, good. Mom wanted me to cut the grass, so I'd hoped I could make it on time." He set his board down and removed his wax from his pocket. "I'm glad to see you brought your longboard today."

"Yep. Looking for an easy ride."

"Need some wax?"

"Nah, I'm ready to go." He rubbed his forehead and stared out at the waves. "How are things going with your folks?"

"Alright. I think I may have misjudged them concerning my return. They were happy to have me home." He shrugged and sighed. "It's still a little awkward, though. We don't really talk all that much. I haven't mentioned the war and they don't bring it up so..."

"Do you want to talk about it?"

"No, not really. But it's good to know I could if I needed to, you know?"

Bobby exhaled and watched as Rick methodically rubbed another layer of wax on his board. "Rick, about Donna..."

Rick looked away. "You have no idea how sorry I am for this whole mess. It was so wrong of me. I just...I have loved Donna for so long. Bobby, you are a lucky man."

"I'd say that I'm probably blessed."

"Do you remember that time we were all at Mack's? It was you, me, and Danny, I think. Anyway, you'd asked me if I digged any girls. Well..."

Bobby nodded. "Donna."

"*Now* you know why I didn't say anything. I wish I could say that I didn't still have feelings for her, but I'd be lying. It's hard to just forget and move on, you know?"

"Oh, I know."

"Listen, I know she's your wife. She belongs to you. I respect that. That's why I encouraged her to go back to you. I don't plan to pursue her, so you can breathe easy."

"I appreciate that, man. We have a rough road ahead of us."

"Yeah, but I have confidence that God can restore relationships."

"I feel like I also need to apologize to you. I said some things that were wrong, and I admit that I wanted to kill you when I found out the truth of the matter."

"You did?" Rick eyed him, probably to see if he was joking again.

He wasn't. "Yes. But I've since forgiven you."

"So you didn't bring out here to knock me off?"

Bobby expelled a burst of laughter. "No, friend. I hoped to make amends."

Rick laughed too. "Oh, good. You had me worried a minute there."

"No need to worry." Bobby strapped his leash to his ankle and picked up his board as Rick did likewise. "You still need to stretch?"

"Nah, the walk over was plenty good enough."

Bobby eyed Rick, then looked out at the vast ocean in front of them. "The first one to catch a wave wins."

"Wins what?" Rick smiled.

"Dinner at Mack's–on the loser?"

"You're on!"

....

Donna pulled a package of sandwich rolls out of the pantry and set them on the table. They'd go perfect with the chicken and corn on the cob that Bobby and Danny were barbequing out on the grill.

"I'm glad you invited us over today." Pamela set the sliced tomatoes, lettuce, and condiments on the table.

"Yeah, me too."

"You look better."

"Thanks." Donna frowned. "I wish I could say that I feel as well as I look."

"Are you still feeling down in the dumps?"

"Not as much as before, but yeah, pretty often."

"Is it mostly because of the babies?"

Donna nodded.

"You know, when Momma died, I wrote her a long letter telling her everything I wished I could have said while she was still alive. All the things I wanted to say but never got the chance. I sealed it up and buried it next to her grave."

Donna frowned.

"It made me feel so much better inside, just to be able to get everything off my chest. I think it lifted a burden." She touched Donna's shoulder. "Do you think that might help you? You could write a letter to your little ones. You know, tell them the things you would have if they were born, as though you were holding them in your arms. You could explain things to them." She shrugged. "I don't know. It helped *me*."

"I think that might be a good idea. It's worth a try, right?"

"Right." Pamela smiled. "You know, one of the things I wrote in my letter is apologizing to Momma that I wasn't more like you."

Donna sneered. "Now, look at me."

Pamela seemingly ignored her comment. "I came to realize that I don't have to be perfect. God made me who I am for a reason only known to Him. Danny showed me that. He said 'I bet Donna has something she's hiding–some deep dark secret.' I laughed at the time."

"Boy, did I."

"But, you know, even David in the Bible sinned big time. He had Bathsheba's husband killed and he had an affair. And *he* was called a man after God's own heart."

"I don't understand that."

"Just because David wasn't perfect, didn't mean that God couldn't use him. God uses imperfect people to fulfill His perfect will. Just look at Rahab, the harlot, and Tamar, who prostituted herself. These are people God chose to be in the direct line of Jesus Christ. I think it's amazing. I don't think that God looks at us and sees our mistakes. I think He looks at us and sees our potential."

"But I know I let Daddy and Momma down."

"All Momma and Daddy wanted from us was to serve God as best as we could. They expected us to mess up. God expects us to mess up. And that's part of why we need Him so much. It's kind of like that song that we sing in church sometimes, *Grace That Is Greater Than All Our Sin*–even the worst ones."

"I think they should hire you as a preacher after Daddy retires."

Pamela slapped her arm in jest. "Oh, stop!"

Donna laughed, but allowed her sister's words to sink in to her thoughts.

Pamela's features twisted in contemplation. "While I'm confessing, I might as well add that I feel kind of...guilty."

"About what?"

"About my babies. With Becky and Jason and now this little one on the way," she touched her slightly-swollen middle, "I just feel...like I'm *too* blessed? I don't know. It almost seems wrong for me to have two healthy babies when yours...didn't make it."

Donna shook her head. "Don't feel bad, Pammy. You can't control what happens."

"I know." Pamela's smile was sad. "I'm sure it's really hard though. Sometimes I wish I could take some of your pain and help you through it."

Her eyes misted. "Thank you, Pammy. That means a lot to me." Donna embraced her sister, breathing in the scent of her hair and breathing out a prayer of thankfulness. *Thank You, God, for a sister and a friend like Pammy.*

Twenty-Three

The door swung open, revealing Daddy, the esteemed Minister Ben Peterson. A smile lit his face. "Donna, Bobby, it's so good to see you!" He offered them both a hug. "Come in, sit down. I was just about to make coffee before devotions. Do you want some?"

Donna looked at Bobby. She wasn't certain how their visit would go, or if they'd even stay long enough for the coffee to stop percolating. It could last two minutes; it could last two hours.

Bobby nodded. "I'll take some."

"Me too, Daddy."

"All right. I'll go get it started." He disappeared into the kitchen and Donna lowered herself onto the sofa, leaving plenty of space for Bobby beside her.

"I don't know if I can do this, Bobby," she whispered.

Her husband's arm stretched across her shoulders and he kissed her temple, then whispered into her ear. "Don't worry, babe. God will help you through this."

"I know He will, I'm just scared. Daddy..." She couldn't go on. The fewer times she voiced her thoughts, the better off she was.

Bobby didn't respond, but simply pressed a kiss to her cheek.

Donna couldn't help her trembling hands, so she attempted to clasp them in her lap. Perhaps Daddy wouldn't notice.

Daddy entered the room and smiled. "You don't know how much pleasure it gives me to see you two in love. Reminds me of my Margaret." Sadness altered his smile as he took a seat in the chair across from them. "So, to what pleasure do I owe this visit?"

Donna glanced at Bobby apprehensively and he nodded.

"I...Bobby and I...need to talk to you." Why did her voice have to come out shaky?

Her father leaned forward, his brow furrowed. "Is something wrong?"

"Yes and no." Tears filled Donna's eyes. "Do you remember that time when I was really sick a few years ago? I was eighteen."

Daddy nodded, pensive.

"I was pregnant."

Her father's eyes widened in surprise and he looked at Bobby, then back at her.

"The baby was Rick's," she clarified.

Daddy leaned back against the recliner. "Rick Landers?"

She nodded.

"I never knew you and Rick..." His eyes darted back and forth from Bobby to her. "What about Bobby? What happened to the baby?"

Donna exhaled and began to explain. "The night of the bonfire on the beach, just after I found out Bobby was cheating on me...that was the night Rick and I... I was so upset and Rick had been so easy to talk to, so kind. I thought I was in love with him."

"And the baby?"

"Rick left for basic training the next day. I didn't know what to do or think. Then I found out I was pregnant. It was right around the time Peggy Walters was expecting. I saw how everyone treated her so badly, heard what they called her. I knew that a baby would change everything. Nobody would ever think of me as a good girl again. I had to be good—I was the preacher's daughter, you know. Your name, Daddy, would be tainted. So I...I had an abortion." Tears blazed a warm path down her cheeks as she studied her father. Bobby's fingers wove into hers, providing an anchor.

"An abortion? You mean you..." Shock, pain, and sorrow rampaged across his features. He covered his face with his hands. "Dear Jesus, no."

The anguish in his voice flayed at her heart. She stood up, and then moved to her father's side, placing an arm around his trembling back. "I'm so sorry. I'm so sorry, Daddy."

Daddy turned and pulled her close, clutching her tightly as they both wept for the precious life they would never know. At least, not in this lifetime.

Bobby offered them tissues, wiping his own eyes as well.

"Why, Donna? Why didn't you come to me?"

"I was afraid of what you'd say. I didn't want to disappoint you. I didn't want to shame our family, your position as the pastor."

Daddy placed his hand atop hers. "None of that matters more than the life of your baby, Donna."

"I know that now. I was so foolish to think it did then. And selfish. My choice cost more than just the life of my baby with Rick, but my two with Bobby as well. The doctor said I miscarried because of damage from the surgery." More tears flooded her eyelids. "I sinned, and then I tried to cover it up. And things just got worse."

"Donna."

She looked up at her father. "Yes?"

"You are forgiven. Jesus forgave you before you even thought of having an abortion. Do you believe that?"

She shoved away her tears and nodded. "I do. But, Daddy, do you think you can forgive me too?"

"I already have, sweetheart." He kissed her forehead. "I already have."

"Do you think my baby's in Heaven with Momma? Even though I–"

"I know it is, honey. And I'm a little jealous that your mother got to meet her three grandchildren before I had a chance."

"I'm sorry, Daddy."

"I'm just happy that we have hope in Christ. Because of Him, we will all see each other someday."

Donna breathed a silent prayer of thanksgiving for the wonderful earthly father God had given her. She couldn't imagine having any other.

Twenty-Four

Bobby took Donna's hand as they prepared to exit the car. "You ready for this?"

She blew out a breath and nodded. "I think so. How about you?"

"I'll be fine. It will probably be more awkward though, with Rick there this time."

"Daddy advised that we all be there to tell his parents. It might be easier for them to hear if Rick is there."

"I know. I hope they take it as well as my folks did."

Tears sprang to Donna's eyes in remembrance of the grace the Dillons had extended to her. "Have I ever told you how wonderful your parents are?"

Bobby smiled. "How do you think I ended up so great?"

Donna laughed and dried her eyes. "Such a clown." She glanced at the Landers' front door. "We should probably go before they come get us."

"Let's pray first."

Donna and Bobby held hands and bowed their heads in unison. "Dear Jesus, please guide us as we break this news to Rick's folks. Give us the words to speak, comfort our hearts, give us peace. Help us to be a comfort to them. And be with them as well. Heal their hurt. Grant them understanding and forgiveness, Lord. And thank You for forgiving us all for our sins. Amen."

"Amen," Donna echoed. She smiled at her beloved husband, marveling again at the grace he continued to display. "Let's go."

They exited the vehicle and approached the front door. Bobby knocked and it swung open a moment later.

"Donna, Bobby, how nice to see you! Ricky told us you would be coming by. Come sit down." Mrs. Landers ushered them into the living room. "Bill just got home from work. I'll go get him." She exited the room, heading down the hallway leading to the bedrooms.

Donna strove not to think about that area of the house. The last time she'd been there...

Rick walked into the living room, providing a much-needed distraction. "Hi, Bobby, Donna. How have you two been?"

Donna suspected he was referring to the state of their marriage.

Bobby spoke first. "Good. Taking it one day at a time."

Donna sensed the bit of tension in her husband's voice. She guessed it was as difficult for him to not think of Rick as competition as it was for her to forget all that had occurred in this house. She squeezed Bobby's hand and sent him a reassuring smile.

Rick took a seat on an empty chair near Bobby. "I'm glad everything's going well."

"It is. Thank you for asking, Rick." Donna glanced around and lowered her voice. "How do you think your parents will respond?"

He frowned. "As you might expect. They'll be upset and disappointed, but..." Rick became silent as his parents joined them.

Mr. Landers extended a hand to Bobby, who stood and shook it. "It's good to see you again, Bobby, Donna. It's been a while since we've talked."

Donna doubted she'd ever had an actual conversation with Rick's father, other than a how-do-you-do at church on Sundays. The Landers most likely thought of her as Danny's sister-in-law and the preacher's daughter. To Donna's knowledge, they knew nothing of her and Rick's relationship.

"Nice to see you too, Mr. Landers. How have you been doing? How's work?"

"Pretty well, thank you. Work is the same as always. Insurance is always a hassle, but we're getting along."

Mrs. Landers placed a hand on her husband's arm. "Bill was just promoted to branch manager."

"That's quite an accomplishment. Congratulations."

Rick's dad shrugged, but was unable to hide a proud smile. "Thank you. Took a long time to get there, but I finally made it. I'm sure you two didn't stop by to hear about my work though."

Bobby's cheerful countenance became solemn. "No, sir, we didn't. Donna and I... Donna, Rick, and I," he corrected himself, "need to speak with you about something important."

Mrs. Landers looked at Rick, then back at Bobby and Donna. "What is it?"

Donna spoke up, clutching her chair tightly as though it provided a lifeline. "When I was eighteen, I became pregnant out of wedlock."

Surprise registered on the Landers' faces and they looked at Rick as though attempting to determine what his part was in the story.

"*I* was the baby's father."

Mrs. Landers gasped at Rick's words, while her husband simply eyed them all in silence.

"Rick left for Vietnam the day after we..." Donna battled the urge to look toward the hallway. Instead, she stared at her hands. "I was alone. I didn't wish to shame my family and I foolishly thought I could fix everything, make my problem go away." A well of tears rose to blur her vision.

"I don't remember you going away." Confusion marked Mrs. Lander's features again.

"I didn't. The doctor...*I* killed my baby. I had an abortion."

"Your baby? Ricky's baby?" Rick's mother looked at him. "You let her have your baby killed? Why didn't you come home and marry her?"

"I didn't know." Rick stared at the floor.

Donna shook her head. "I didn't tell him I was expecting. I wrote him a letter, but I couldn't put anything specific in it."

Regret registered on Rick's face as though he had just realized why she'd written to him.

"So you...you just *killed* the baby? Why didn't you tell us? We would have wanted Rick's baby. We would have kept it."

"I didn't want to shame or disappoint anyone. It seemed like the only thing I could do." Donna wiped the tears off her face. "I'm so sorry. Please forgive me."

Mrs. Landers began to shake and moisture sparkled in her eyes. "Forgive you for murdering our grandbaby? How can you expect us to forgive you?" She stood up and paced the room "This is not acceptable at all."

Rick rushed to his mother. "Mom, there has already been enough heartache."

"But she should have told us!" She pointed a finger at Donna.

"Mom, listen to me. It was *my* baby too." The emotion in Rick's voice prompted a fresh wave of tears, blurring Donna's vision. "If anyone should be upset with Donna for this, it's *me*. And I can't say that I wasn't upset when she first told me. But she doesn't need condemnation, she needs forgiveness. If I can forgive Donna, you can too."

She turned to her husband. "Bill, say something."

Mr. Landers studied them all, then turned to Bobby. "You have forgiven your wife for doing this? And my son, for his part?"

Bobby nodded. "I'm far from innocent, sir. You see, I wasn't faithful to Donna when we dated. I had another girl. The night Donna and Rick sinned...that was after Donna found out that I'd been cheating on her. I am no less guilty than they are.

"From how I see it, sir, none of us are innocent. We have

all sinned in God's sight. None of us deserve forgiveness. And yet, we have *all* been forgiven." He briefly glanced toward Mrs. Landers. "To refuse to forgive wrongs against me when my wrongs against Christ nailed Him to the cross would be placing myself above God. It isn't easy to forgive, but it's what's right. Jesus gave me the strength to do what is right." Bobby placed his arm around Donna. "And I wouldn't have Donna as my wife if I hadn't forgiven her and Rick."

Mr. Landers nodded and looked at his wife. "Perhaps we should be glad our son did not have a child out-of-wedlock. Not that Donna's behavior is acceptable, but think about it." He then met Donna's gaze. "Nobody knows about this, right?"

Donna shook her head. "We told my father yesterday, and Pammy and Danny know."

He nodded. "Please give us time to process this news. As you can imagine, we're a little stunned right now. We will see you in church on Sunday." He beckoned to his wife and she reluctantly returned to his side.

Donna nodded, unsure of what to say.

Bobby stood and Donna followed him to the door.

Rick joined them outside. "Don't worry, my parents will come around. They're just pretty shocked about all of this. Probably thought I was almost perfect." He winced.

"God will work it out." Bobby clasped Rick's shoulder.

The still-evident, although strained, camaraderie between them warmed Donna's heart. If Bobby and Rick could still consider each other friends after all that had happened, anything was possible.

"Pammy gave me an idea last night, to write letters."

Rick frowned. "Letters?"

Donna nodded. "Letters to the children we've lost. My baby with you, Rick. And my two with Bobby." She glanced at her husband. "We can put our letters in a box and bury them in the graveyard, where Robert Jr. is, maybe? I thought it would be good if Daddy could be there too."

As Bobby and Rick considered the idea, Donna added, "I think it would be healing. For all of us."

Bobby nodded. "Okay. We can do that. When would we bury the letters?"

"Would Saturday work? At eleven? I'm sure it will be fine for Daddy."

Rick nodded. "I'll be there."

....

Donna entered the dining room where Bobby sat quietly with his head in his hands. His Bible lay open on the table in front of him. *Is he praying?* The last thing Donna wished to do was disturb him, so she turned around to go back to the bedroom and allow him the privacy he needed.

"Donna," his hoarse voice called out.

She turned and at that moment noticed the tears in his eyes. "Bobby, what's wrong?" She went to him.

"Sit, please."

She did as requested and waited in silence for him to say whatever it was he needed to say.

He looked up, his gaze penetrated hers, but the brokenness she found there was haunting. "I...I need to ask you something."

"Okay."

He lowered his gaze and now stared at his hands. "You loved Rick. You hoped to marry him, but you got stuck with me. I mean, if he hadn't gone off to Vietnam, you two would be married now. I can't help thinking in my mind that you'd rather be with him. I know he'd rather be with you."

Why is he bringing this up? "Bobby, that's in the past."

"Donna, would you rather be with Rick?" His stare demanded nothing but the truth.

Why would he ask this question? "No."

He shook his head. "I don't think that's true."

"Well, it is. It's also true that I loved Rick. I admit that. But I did marry *you*. Bobby, I was engaged to you and planned to marry *you* first, remember?"

"Yes. I guess I just feel unworthy. Like, yes, I have you as my wife but I really shouldn't. I mean, if you and Rick shared this incredible bond, who was I to step in and marry you while your heart belonged to someone else?"

"When Daddy came to me and asked me if I'd forgiven you, I already had. When he asked if I'd consider marrying you, I had already determined my relationship with Rick was over."

"Great. So you married me to please your father."

"No, Bobby. I married you because I love you. Not for any other reason. If anyone is unworthy of this marriage, it's me, not you. I have made so many mistakes already. Now, I just want to move on. I don't want to dwell on the past any longer."

There was so much more she could say. Like how it felt like a giant weight crushed her chest every time she thought of the mistakes she'd make and the hurt she'd brought to others. Like how it pained her to look into Rick's or Bobby's eyes knowing she'd been responsible for snuffing out the lives of their precious babies.

The words of Rick's mother came back to haunt her once again. *She didn't deserve forgiveness.* It was true. Maybe she shouldn't be forgiven. If she wasn't, maybe a portion of this guilt would somehow lift from her shoulders. But unforgiveness would never bring back her babies. It would not raise them from the dead. Forgiving herself was her only chance at relief, yet she found the task *so* difficult. But she *had to* move on, because if she didn't she was certain this cloud of darkness would envelop her and eventually pour down so much rain it would completely drown her.

....

The task proved more difficult than Donna imagined. She wondered how the guys were faring with their letters. Alas, she had finished the last and most difficult letter of all – the one to her and Rick's baby – the innocent life she'd purposely cut short. She swiped another tear as she silently reread her letter one last time.

> *To my sweet baby,*
> *Oh, dear precious one! You may not know me, but I am your Momma. I look forward to the day we can meet face to face.*

I want to say that I hope you're happy up in Heaven with Jesus. I know it must be wonderful up there. I'm sure you've already met your brother and sister. And your grandma. I bet she was so excited to see you. I know she must love you very much. Your daddy and I love you very much too, but we never had a chance to show you. That was Momma's fault.

I'm so sorry for ending your life. If there is anything in my life that I could go back and undo, that would be it. I'm sorry that I was selfish and valued myself and my life above yours. I'm sorry that I caused you pain. I'm sorry that I didn't love and cherish you as a mother should. I'm sorry that I'll never know you this side of Heaven.

Please forgive me.

One day I hope to give you the love that you should have had here on this earth. I look forward to the day I can hold you in my arms. If only I could do that now...

I know that I can't, but because of what Jesus did for me, I know I will see you in Heaven one day.

Goodbye, Precious!

All my love,

Momma

Donna finally folded the letter and brought it to her lips and kissed it, then grieved once again for the babies she'd never know this side of Heaven.

....

Robert William Dillon Jr.
March 4, 1970 – March 4, 1970

Bobby stared down at the tiny tombstone. It was hard to believe that it'd been almost a year since he'd held his sweet little boy in his arms, touched his tiny lifeless face. He knew the ache in his heart would never go away, the deep craving to have the opportunity to know his children would never be satisfied. Not in this lifetime, at least.

A sniffle beside him drew his attention to his wife. Donna had been through so much. Bobby knew for a fact that her pain was infinitely heavier than his own, for she carried the weight of her guilt. He wrapped an arm around her waist, allowing her to lean her head on his shoulder. He kissed the top of her head and whispered into her hair, "I love you."

A bittersweet silence surrounded them, sweet for the love they shared, and bitter for the loss they also shared. Donna straightened and met Bobby's gaze. "I can't wait to meet them someday."

He smiled, doing his best to shove down the lump in his throat. "Me too."

His attention was diverted by the arrival of Donna's father, followed by Rick. As they approached, Bobby noticed the envelope in Rick's hand and the wooden box in Preacher Peterson's.

He extended the box to Donna. "I thought we could bury the letters in here."

"Momma's treasure chest? Daddy, no. We can't use that."

The minister nodded. "You can. She would have wanted you to use it."

Tears sparkled in Donna's eyes as she accepted it. "Thank you." She opened the box and placed her letters inside. Rick stepped forward and handed over his envelope as Bobby pulled his out of his back pocket. Bobby had written two letters, one to Robert Jr. and another to their second baby. He'd considered penning a letter to Rick and Donna's baby as well but hadn't known what to say. He wondered if Rick had written more than the one letter to his and Donna's child.

Donna closed the box and Bobby reached for his shovel. He planted the blade into the ground and dug a small hole. Donna knelt and kissed the box before laying it to rest in the dirt. "I love you, my precious babies." She rose to her feet and Bobby drew her to his side.

Preacher Peterson stepped forward and they all bowed their heads. "Dear Lord, we place these letters, along with the three precious souls they're written to, into Your care. I pray that the words contained in these letters have brought healing to Bobby, Donna, and Rick. Please overwhelm them with Your comfort, Lord. Let them never doubt Your presence and purpose in their lives. Guide each of them with Your mighty hand. We thank You for Your infinite mercy and grace that You continue to show us every day. Remind us daily of Your love and forgiveness. We praise You alone, Jesus.

"Though we didn't have the chance to know these precious children in this life, we look forward to the day when we will. Until then, comfort our hearts. We entrust them to You, Father. In Your holy name, amen."

"Amen," Bobby, Donna, and Rick echoed. Bobby handed Rick the shovel and he dumped earth onto the wooden box until all sign of it was gone.

Twenty-Five

Ben Peterson approached his daughter and asked for a private audience near the front of the church.

She nodded and let Bobby know she'd catch up to him shortly after speaking with her father. "You wanted to speak with me, Daddy?"

"Yes, sweetheart. How are you holding up?"

"Okay, I guess." She shrugged.

"You look sad." He met her eyes.

"I know in my head that Jesus has forgiven me, Daddy. I just can't seem to make my heart understand it." She frowned.

"Donna, those seeds of doubt come from the devil. He is a liar. His goal is to kill, steal, and destroy. He doesn't want you to have joy because he knows that if you do, you will move out of this pit of defeat and do something great for God."

"I want to have joy again, Daddy."

"Then resist the devil and he will flee from you. Draw nigh to God and He will draw nigh to you. Trust God and take Him at His Word, Donna. This is the only way you can live in victory." He rubbed her back. "You have been hit hard. But a just man falleth seven times, yet riseth up again. It will be a daily battle, but it's one you must win if you want freedom. His Word says that if you confess and forsake your sin, you will find mercy. Believe it. Turn to God, Donna. He is there with you every minute of the day–even when the devil tells you He is not."

She stood on her tiptoes and kissed his cheek. "Thank you, Daddy. That's exactly what I needed to hear. I think I might write some of those verses down and read them every day to remind myself."

"That's a great idea, sweetheart." He smiled. "Well, I bet Bobby's probably ready to go now, huh?"

"Do you want to come over and have dinner with us, Daddy?"

"It's awfully tempting, but I'm looking forward to a nice nap today."

"Okay, maybe next week then?"

"Next week sounds wonderful, sweetheart."

....

Rick strode down the church steps, momentarily closed his eyes, and bathed in the warm sunshine.

"Rick."

His eyes popped open.

Preacher Peterson approached him and peered over his reading glasses, still perched on the bridge of his nose from his Sunday sermon reading. "There's something I'd like to discuss with you."

Oh, no. Time to face the music. He knew that Preacher Peterson would eventually reprimand him for his and Donna's misdeed. Rick wiped his hands on his pants. Why were they clammy all of a sudden?

Rick swallowed. "Yes, sir?"

"Would you meet me in my office in a few moments, please? I just need to speak with Pamela before she leaves. It's open. You may go ahead and take a seat. I'll be right there."

He noted the serious tone in the preacher's voice and inwardly cringed. This was not a conversation he was looking forward to. At all.

"Sure." Rick walked to the preacher's office, which was just behind the front platform in the church. He sat down in the chair across from the preacher's desk, tapping his fingers on his trousers. He took a couple of deep breaths and attempted to mentally brace himself. He couldn't just sit there and do nothing, so he sprung up and analyzed the bookcase behind him.

"You like to read?"

Rick jumped and turned at the pastor's voice.

"Sorry, I didn't mean to startle you."

"Oh, no. It's okay. I was just lost in thought."

"Yeah, I do that sometimes too." Preacher Peterson smiled. "Do you know why I asked you to join me?"

To chastise me for causing your daughter so much heartache? Rick loosened his collar. "Uh, no, sir. Not exactly." He gulped in another gallon of air.

"I received a letter the other day from our missionaries.

The Johnson family. Do you remember them?" He reached into his top drawer as he sat down across the desk.

What? What does this have to do with me and Donna? Rick blinked, refocusing his tempestuous thoughts. "They're the ones in Mexico?"

"Yes, that's the Johnsons." He unfolded the letter and handed it to Rick.

Rick scanned it quickly, still confused. *What on earth does this have to do with me?*

"The reason I wanted to speak with you is I think you would do well on the mission field. The Johnsons are asking for help. They're building a church and a school down there and I thought maybe you might be interested in something like that."

"Oh."

"Of course, you'd need to pray about it and I'm thinking you'll want to discuss it with your folks."

"Yes, of course." Rick nodded, still attempting to process what the preacher said.

"Well, that's all. I thought of all our congregants and the Lord brought you to mind." He stood from his desk and sat on the corner.

"I...I don't know what to say." Rick's eyes misted. "I mean, do you think the Lord can use someone like me?"

Preacher Peterson reached over and clasped his shoulder. "God *especially* uses people like you. Rick, no one is perfect. And God already knows that."

"I admit that I thought you called me in here to confront me about my relationship with Donna."

The preacher frowned. "That's already been forgiven. It's in the past where it needs to stay. We just need to learn from our mistakes so we don't make the same ones again." A corner of his mouth rose. "Let's all move on now and see if God doesn't have a wonderful future planned for us, shall we?"

Rick nodded. "Thank you for your words of encouragement, Pastor."

Preacher Peterson shook his hand. "You're welcome, Rick."

....

"I'd like Rick Landers to come to the front, please." Preacher Peterson announced from the pulpit.

Rick's hands were sweating, but he did as the preacher bade and went and stood just below the pulpit.

The preacher joined him and put an arm around his shoulders. He looked out at the congregation. "If you've been in this church very long at all, you know the Landers family have been faithful members. Rick, here, will be leaving for the mission field in Mexico this week."

A few gasps escaped around the room.

"I'd like us all to come up to the front and show our support for Rick by laying hands on him in prayer. And if you wanted to drop a dollar bill or two into his pocket, I'm sure he wouldn't mind that either."

Rick heard a few chuckles, but took a deep breath as the congregation moved forward and began laying their hands on him. His eyes began to mist as, one by one, and all at once, his family in Christ began to pray for his departure.

It would be bittersweet. He'd certainly miss his family and friends here in California, but he was excited about doing God's work down in Mexico. It would feel good to get his mind off of himself and his problems for once and be able to help others out.

He felt a firm hand on his shoulder and glanced back to see Bobby. His friend nodded and Rick mouthed, "Thanks, man." He was certain that Bobby had no idea how great it felt to have his support after all they'd been through.

Twenty-Six

The following year...

Ben Peterson looked down at the sleeping baby in his arms and smiled in amazement. No matter how many times he held a precious new life, he'd never get over God's graciousness to mankind and the miracle of life itself.

"Do you need me to take her, Daddy?"

He glanced up at his eldest daughter and couldn't help but remember when she'd been at this stage in life. Small, innocent, and helpless. But now, here she was, not only grown up with a small family of her own but with hard-earned wisdom that could only be culminated through the trials of life. And trials she'd had. "No, Donna. She's just fine."

"She looks like Momma, doesn't she?"

"Somewhat, I suppose. But I really think she favors Bobby. At least, she has his nose."

Donna smiled and sat down next to him on the couch. "She does, doesn't she? I'm still in awe that God would bless me with a baby after all I've done. The doctor said she's definitely a miracle baby."

"Remember, Donna. God's goodness doesn't depend on us. God *is* good. It's one of His characteristics." He grinned as he stroked the baby's hand. "And while I believe *every* baby is a miracle, little Jamie *especially* is."

He reached an arm around his eldest daughter. "Your momma is probably looking down from Heaven and smiling, I'm sure."

"I hope so. But I still miss her and think about her every day."

"Me too, Donna. Me too." He gently lifted his granddaughter and placed her in her mother's arms. He moved to his office and pulled out the letter he'd received from Mexico.

"I have something that I'd like to show all of you. It came in the mail this week."

He looked around the room and took in the family the Good Lord had blessed him with–Donna and Robert and their sweet young daughter, Pamela and Daniel and their three children who seemed to grow each time he saw them. It was a blessing indeed to have them here in his and Margaret's house, sharing a Saturday afternoon meal, visiting and enjoying each other's company.

"I plan to share this letter with the congregation tomorrow, but there is something in here that is especially for our family. I wanted all of you to be present because of this. I'll read it to you." He opened the envelope and pulled out a piece of lined paper. *"Note: Preacher Peterson, please read this letter to the congregation but be sure that Donna and Bobby and my family get to see the picture. The photo is to be kept private, between my family and yours, please."*

Bobby now held their baby as Donna sat forward on the couch. "Where's the picture?"

Ben smiled. "Patience, daughter. Let me read the letter first."

Donna nodded and glanced at Bobby.

"*Dear Brothers and Sisters in Christ,*

Hola, amigos! (That's 'Hello, friends!' in Spanish) I can't express my thankfulness of your support throughout the last year. We've accomplished much here in Mexico, by the grace of God. We've built a small church and school, where our Mexican brothers and sisters meet almost daily, and we've seen many souls come to Christ.

I have learned some Spanish and Bro. Johnson has had me preaching in services here and there. I admit that I'm not that good at it, but the brothers and sisters here are gracious and tell me that they've been able to understand my words.

Another thing we've built here is an orphanage. There are so many homeless children here, it was definitely needed. We're also teaching some adults to read.

Well, there's much work to be done so I'll close for now. I miss you all. Thanks again for your support. Please continue to keep me and the Johnsons and the Gonzalez

family (Senor González is a local pastor) in your prayers.
Adiós, mis amigos! (Goodbye, my friends!)
In Christ alone,
Rick Landers"

"Wow! It sounds like he's been pretty busy over there." Bobby lightly rubbed the baby's back.

Danny spoke this time. "They've built a church, a school, and an orphanage all in a year? That's amazing."

Ben smiled. "Yes, I believe it was God's prompting that encouraged me to mention Mexico to Rick. It seems to suit him."

Pamela approached him and asked to see the letter. "You said he sent a photo too?"

"Oh, yes. Here it is." He pulled the photo from the envelope and handed it to Pamela.

"Oh, my goodness! Donna, look at this." Pamela smiled and gave the photo to Bobby and Donna. They all came and gathered around the divan to view the photo simultaneously.

"*In loving memory of Robert Dillon, Jr., Margaret Dillon, and Baby Landers.*" Donna read the words on a plaque held by Rick in the photo. She flipped the photo over and read the words he'd written on the back.

"*Bobby and Donna, I thought this would be a special way to remember the little ones we've lost. I hope you're okay with this. The plaque is on the front of the orphanage now and is a daily reminder to me of God's grace.*"

Ben looked to Bobby, whose eyes seem to haze just a

little. He would cherish the sentimental moment in his heart all his days. The way God had worked to bring healing in his family was more wonderful than he ever could have imagined.

Twenty-Seven

Spring 1972...

"Please stand and turn in your Bibles to Romans, chapter eight."

A small commotion from the back of the sanctuary itched Donna's curiosity but she refused to look. Growing up as a preacher's daughter, she'd learned early to keep her focus on the speaker and not to gawk about. It had taken her years to overcome the constant temptation to see what was happening, but she'd finally gotten a hold of her curiosity.

Bobby, on the other hand, obviously hadn't. "Donna, look."

Puzzled at her husband's tone, she turned and gasped. "Rick's back."

Rick, who had apparently just entered the church building, was making his way to an empty seat. A pretty young woman followed close behind him.

"I wonder who that is with him."

Donna glanced up and caught Bobby's grin. "My guess is he's found himself a girlfriend," he said.

She smiled. "Could be."

Daddy drew their attention to the pulpit and Donna did her best to concentrate on the sermon while questions flitted through her mind. After the invitation, Daddy pulled Rick's letter out of his pocket. "Today, I planned to read a letter from one of our missionaries about the work that has been accomplished in Mexico, but I see that he can tell you all about it himself. Rick Landers, would you please come to the front?"

A friendly smile adorning his face, Rick strode up the aisle and offered her father a half-hug. "Thank you, sir." As Daddy took a seat in the front row, Rick turned to face the congregation. "I am so grateful to be back amongst friends and family once again." His gaze met Donna's, then shifted to Bobby. "Thank you all for your support in this past year. Your prayers have not been in vain."

As Rick explained all that had occurred in the past twelve months, Donna studied him. It became increasingly clear that the mission field had changed him. Donna almost felt as though she was seeing a new Rick, one who was more confident, strong in his faith, ready to help in any situation. He had grown a lot in the past year, something she and Bobby could both identify with.

During her pregnancy with Jamie, Donna had found all of her old fears and doubts resurfacing. She'd prayed for a healthy child as she battled her sense of unworthiness and she struggled to trust God with her baby's life. Speaking with Bobby, she discovered that he'd been experiencing the same thing and they strove together to seek the Lord's guidance. It had been a struggle, but they'd slowly learned to lift their concerns to God and give Him all control.

It pleased Donna to see that Rick had accomplished the same thing.

Fifteen minutes later, Bobby and Donna approached Rick.

"Rick, it's so great to see you!" Bobby wrapped him in a bear hug.

"You too, man." Rick smiled at Donna and gave her a hug. He stepped back and eyed them both. "So, how've you two been?"

"Great. God has definitely blessed us."

Donna retrieved Jamie from Pammy's arms and held her up. "This is our daughter, Jamie."

Joy lit Rick's eyes. "She's so beautiful. Your father mentioned you were expecting in one of his letters."

"We named her after Daddy actually. James is his middle name."

Rick brushed his finger across Jamie's hand and she latched onto him. "She's precious. How old is she?"

"Three months." There was more than a hint of pride in Bobby's voice as they all admired his baby girl.

"She's tiny."

Donna looked up at the unfamiliar voice and met the brown-eyed gaze of the woman who had arrived with Rick.

"Rick, you want to introduce us to your friend?" Bobby teased.

"Ah, she's more than a friend." Rick grinned and placed an arm around the young woman's shoulders. "You aren't the only one who has been blessed. Meet Sue Johnson, my fiancé."

As Bobby congratulated Rick, Donna's eyes widened at the name. "Sue Johnson? Suzy? Do you remember me? You, Pammy, and I used to make sandcastles together when, before your family moved to Mexico. What were we, like five or six?"

A smile lit her face. "Yes, I do remember. We had so much fun. Such good memories. I guess we would have been about five or so because I was seven when we moved." Sue embraced her. "It's wonderful to see you again, Donna."

"You too. It seems like such a long time since I last saw you. Wow." Donna smiled as Sue stepped back to Rick's side. "Wait a minute, you said your fiancé? Rick, you and Sue are engaged? To be married?"

Rick and Sue nodded simultaneously.

"That's wonderful! Congratulations! Do you have a date set?"

Sue turned to Rick, who spoke, "Actually, that was something we wanted to discuss with your father. If it's fine with him, we'd like to get married today."

"*Today*?" Donna and Bobby asked at the same time.

Rick nodded with a grin and Sue clung to his arm. "Sue's parents will be driving up here this afternoon. They couldn't leave until after the church service."

"We decided to come back here for our wedding, since we were both raised in this church, and Rick especially wanted you two," Sue's gaze flicked from Donna to Bobby, "to be there when we get married."

Bobby smiled at Rick. "I'm honored."

"There's more." Rick's countenance grew serious. "If you

don't mind, man, I'd love it if you would be my best man."

Bobby's smile trembled a bit, the barely-noticeable action evoking tears in Donna's eyes. "I consider that one of the greatest honors I've ever received. I accept."

Rick grinned. "Thank you."

Sue turned to Donna. "And Donna, would you be my matron of honor?"

"Me?"

Sue nodded. "I don't have any sisters to ask and my friend in Mexico will be unable to come. I have always known you as a friend. I would like to have you and Pamela stand with me, if you will."

"And I'm hoping my brother will be a groomsman," Rick added.

"That's... Wow. Yes, yes, I accept. Thank you for asking me, Sue."

A sweet smile grew on her face. "It was my pleasure, Donna."

Rick took Sue's hand. "If you two don't mind, Sue and I need to go speak with Preacher Peterson and make sure we can actually get married today."

"Of course. Go ahead. And congratulations to you both." Bobby smiled.

As Rick and Sue approached Daddy, hand-in-hand, Bobby and Donna turned to each other and smiled. "Wow."

....

Rick took a deep breath as he stood at the front of the church he'd grown up in. The many times over the years he'd pictured this day in his mind, he'd always pictured Donna walking up the aisle toward him.

And so she was today, but not at his bride. Somehow though, the thought didn't sadden him as it would have a year ago.

He met her gaze as she walked toward the front and he imagined an unspoken communication between them. Donna's gaze then flitted to Bobby and he sent up a prayer of thanksgiving for his best friend. The fact that they could stand side by side today was, without a doubt, a miracle.

Donna still held a piece of his heart and always would, he wouldn't deny that. For memories could be suppressed, but never truly forgotten. They'd shared something that had been real, but it wasn't meant to be.

However, God knew best, and Rick had no doubt that He had put him and Sue together.

Sue.

Now, his bride stood at the back of the church.

The congregation rose as she began her assent to the platform, while the pianist played the familiar wedding march.

Rick couldn't take his eyes off her. This woman–this beautiful, loving, God-fearing young woman was about to become his wife. He'd never get over the fact that she said yes. Even with his tarnished past, his imperfections and inadequacies, she'd happily agreed to become his life-long partner to love, honor, and cherish. The fact truly humbled him. They'd had an amazing year together. Rick couldn't wait to see what God had in store for their future.

This day marked a new chapter in his life, a chapter filled with new hopes and dreams. It was a chapter only a loving God could write.

Epilogue

While it may have happened many years ago, in my heart it feels like just yesterday. I've learned not to take anything for granted – that each day is a precious gift and tomorrow is not promised. I do not know what I would have done without hope in the eternal – that *someday* we will see our loved ones again. I continue to be amazed at God's goodness toward me. I truly don't know how I would have survived without His hand guiding me, without His wonderful love and redeeming grace. And yet, I was the innocent one...

The End

Publisher's Note

If you've read the book, *An Unforgivable Secret* (*Amish Secrets* #1) by J.E.B. Spredemann, there's no doubt you recognized the resemblances to this book. Although the books are vastly different in some areas, in other places there are stark similarities. This is on purpose. We felt the truths in this book were so valuable, we didn't want to limit them to readers of the Amish genre only. We hope you have enjoyed this derivative work and have gained insight into one of the most controversial topics of our day, as well as a better understanding of God's unfailing grace.

If you'd like to contact the authors, you may reach them here:
blessedpublishing1@gmail.com

Did you enjoy the book?
We'd love to hear your thoughts on it.
Reviews are helpful to readers *and* authors
and are greatly appreciated!

Thank you for reading!

Discussion Questions for *If He Only Knew*

(All Scripture references are taken from the *King James Version* of the Holy Bible.)

1. Without disclosing what the secret is (for those who may not have finished reading the book), did you have any idea what Donna's secret might be prior to the revelation?

2. We see in Psalm 44:21, there really is no such thing as a secret, at least, not before God. The verse states, '*Shall not God search this out? For he knoweth the secrets of the heart.*' What does this verse mean to you?

3. What did you think of Pamela at the onset of the story? Did your opinion of her change by the end? Why?

4. When Rick discovered that his best friend had been unfaithful to his girl, do you think he was right in not revealing Bobby's secret? Why or why not? If possible, back up your answer with Scripture. (See Notes) Ch. 3

5. In Chapter Five, after learning of Bobby's misdeed, Donna was distraught. Have you ever made an irrational decision based on your emotions? (See Notes)

6. Fear can be a powerful motivator. This book deals with fear in many instances: Donna made an unwise, life-altering decision because of fear, and continued to hide it because of fear, and the list goes on. Have you ever acted out of fear? How did this impact your life? (See Notes)

7. A popular quote from the book states that '*With Jesus in his heart, he was never, and would never, be alone.*' Do you know this to be true in your own life? Ch. 18

8. At one point, Pamela mentions that she experienced feelings of guilt that she and Danny had two healthy children. Have you ever experienced a similar situation? Or, perhaps you've been on the opposite end. How did you feel when hearing someone else's news in light of your own misfortune? (Note: If you feel this question is too personal, you don't need to answer. However, your answer could help someone in dealing with their current situation, or help others know how to respond if the situation arises again.) Ch. 22

9. Did you think Rick's reaction to Donna's revelation was justified? What about Donna's response to Rick? Ch. 17

10. Did you think Bobby's reaction to Rick was justified? His response to Donna? How could the situation be resolved in a better way? (See notes) Ch. 17

11. When Pamela realized that Donna had carried this secret burden alone for years, she wondered how many others also suffered in silence. Have you ever contemplated this? As humans, we often get wrapped up in our own lives and fail to see others around us who may be struggling. How can we help others who might be going through a situation similar to Donna's? Ch. 20

12. In retrospect, what do you think would have happened if Donna would have told Rick about her circumstances in the first place? How would this have altered each of their lives?

13. In what ways did Donna facilitate healing in her life?

14. What life lessons did you learn from this book? Do you feel the book drew you closer to God? Why or why not?

15. Who was your favorite character and why?

16. Was there a particular Scripture verse or quote that spoke to your heart? Please share.

Thanks for reading!

KJV Scriptures used in this Discussion Guide:

Q.2 Psalm 44:21 Shall not God search this out? for he knoweth the secrets of the heart.

Q.4 Proverbs 26:17 He that passeth by, *and* meddleth with strife *belonging* not to him, *is like* one that taketh a dog by the ears.

Matthew 7:12 Therefore all things whatsoever ye would that men should do to you, do ye even so to them: for this is the law and the prophets.

Q.5 Proverbs 4:23 Keep thy heart with all diligence; for out of it *are* the issues of life.

Jeremiah 17:9 The heart *is* deceitful above all *things*, and desperately wicked: who can know it?

Q.6 Deuteronomy 31:6 Be strong and of a good courage, fear not, nor be afraid of them: for the LORD thy God, he *it is* that doth go with thee; he will not fail thee, nor forsake thee.

1Samuel 12:20 And Samuel said unto the people, Fear not: ye have done all this wickedness: yet turn not aside from following the LORD, but serve the LORD with all your heart;

Psalm 27:1 The LORD *is* my light and my salvation; whom shall I fear? the LORD *is* the strength of my life; of whom shall I be afraid?

Isaiah 41:10 Fear thou not; for I *am* with thee: be not

dismayed; for I *am* thy God: I will strengthen thee; yea, I will help thee; yea, I will uphold thee with the right hand of my righteousness.

2Timothy 1:7 For God hath not given us the spirit of fear; but of power, and of love, and of a sound mind.

Q.10 Proverbs 12:18 There is that speaketh like the piercings of a sword: but the tongue of the wise *is* health.

Proverbs 18:21 Death and life *are* in the power of the tongue: and they that love it shall eat the fruit thereof.

Proverbs 21:23 Whoso keepeth his mouth and his tongue keepeth his soul from troubles.